THE GAME OF
MOUNTAIN AND CHANCE

THE GAME OF MOUNTAIN AND CHANCE

STORIES ABOUT MOUNTAINS
AND MOUNTAINEERS
BY ANNE SAUVY

BÂTON WICKS · LONDON

Also by Anne Sauvy:

FLAMMES DE PIERRE
(Diadem 1991, now available from Bâton Wicks.
Éditions Montalba, Paris, 1982;
Presses Universitaires de Grenoble, 1993)

LE JEU DE LA MONTAGNE ET DU HASARD
(Éditions Montalba, Paris, 1985;
Presses Universitaires de Grenoble, 1995)

LA TÉNÈBRE ET L'AZUR
(Les Éditions Arthaud, Paris, 1991)

NADIR (Éditions Glénat, Grenoble, 1995)

Copyright © by Anne Sauvy

Published in Great Britain in 1995
by Bâton Wicks, London

First published in France in 1985 as
Le jeu de la montagne et du hasard
by Éditions Montalba, Paris

Trade enquiries: Cordee, 3a De Montfort Street, Leicester LE1 7HD

British Cataloguing-in-Publication Data
A catalogue record for this book is available from the British Library.
ISBN 0-898573-15-8

Printed and bound in Great Britain by
Biddles Ltd., Guildford and Kings Lynn

CONTENTS

To the memory of my parents,
Marthe and Alfred Sauvy

PREFACE

Writing a book is something of an adventure. The author leaves a well-known world for another, one completely desert and wild, which he has to shape, organize and in the end dominate. Or at least that is the idea. But having a book translated is also an adventure, possibly even more hazardous and difficult, especially if the writer has some notion, however faint, of the language concerned.

I have published three collections of mountaineering stories *Les flammes de pierre*, *Le jeu de la montagne et du hasard*, *La Ténèbre et l'azur*, and a novel, *Nadir*. The first was published in English in 1990 is now going to be translated into Czech, but that is not really a problem for me because I have absolutely no knowledge of Czech. Perhaps there will be mistakes in it? I shall simply not know about them. But English! When one's husband is English!

In this book, the names of the translators will not be indicated, because it is in some way a collective labour. Anthea Bell was the main translator, but in part she reviewed earlier translations of some of the stories by Professor Ernst Sondheimer and one by Sir Edward Peck, each of which had already been revised by my husband, John C. Wilkinson. John and I then reread the whole collection, checking for details and climbing terms. Anthea Bell incorporated our modifications, and we had another look through. Then my publisher made some suggestions so that more changes were made and further revision followed. Inevitably there will be shortcomings, but it is to be hoped that after all this work the text reads well, for a great deal more effort has been put into it than is generally the case when a book is translated from one language into another. I should like to thank all those who helped prepare this English edition.

There are sixteen stories in *The Game of Mountain and Chance*, in the same pattern my first book in English – *Flammes de Pierre*. I feel the short story genre is particularly suitable for the mountaineering setting as it permits a range of approaches, each story a self-sufficient tale conveying humour, drama, fantasy, or what have you, expressed succinctly and often with its own final twist. It is because I have so much enjoyed reading short stories, from de Maupassant to Fredric Brown, that I have been inspired to try and write them myself.

The title of this book, which is also the title of one of the tales, refers to a well-known XVIIIth century French play, *The Game of Love and Chance*. And where is chance more important than in the mountains?

The opening story, "The Bronze Mountaineers", is a fantasy in which the Chamonix statues of Balmat and de Saussure manage to escape to the heights to reclimb the summit of Mont Blanc, whose first ascent they did, two hundred years ago. So too is "A True Story", except this is not make-believe, but a real event as recounted to me directly. But "The Ice Fairy" and "A Tour of the Massif" are just humorous inventions, the second being something of a skit on archeological reconstructions, ap- plied to the Chamonix Valley. Some of the stories are straight narrative, as for example "The Veteran", which poses the painful problem for ageing climbers of recognising there may be a moment to stop. My stories are pure fiction and not at all autobiographical, but of course there is always some link with a world which only the author knows. The origins of "My Unknown Friend" go back to a personal memory. When I was eighteen, I met a British climber of about my age in Chamonix, called Peter, who was returning to England in an hour's time. As we chatted we found we had the same outlook about moun- taineering. Probably we planned to climb together, the following year. Anyhow, it was a very warm and friendly discussion, which stuck with me. When I came back, some months after, to the students' chalet where we had met, the first question the landlady asked me was: 'Did you know Peter?' In such a way did I learn he was dead. Climbing. In Scotland. Many years later, turning over the pages of an old *Climbers' Club Journal*, I came across his obituary and discovered his full name, Peter Drummond Smith, along with some account of his short life, his studies, his character. It was that impression which inspired this story, quite different, yet of the same ilk, and why I dedicated it to him, my nearly unknown friend.

And I dedicate it also to Georges Bettembourg whom I met in 1983. My friend Jean-Franck Charlet had told me that Georges admired my stories. Jean-Franck finally brought us together at the Crystal Fair in Chamonix and it rapidly became clear that we had much in common with our love of the mountains and literature. But, just one week later,

Georges was killed by a rockfall while crystal hunting on the Aiguille Verte – my second nearly unknown friend.

So, each story has its own story, albeit completely reinvented for fiction. But there is always a small link with something real, even in "Carmencita", which looks like total fancy. And to tell the truth, that is the great moment for an author, the pure climax, when suddenly an idea, a phrase, a little detail from the true world develops into something completely fictitious, fabulous, powerful. Then comes the task of writing, fighting with words; the efforts of translating. But that is another story …

ANNE SAUVY Paris, 1995

THE BRONZE MOUNTAINEERS

During the hundred years they had stood there perched on their block of granite, now one side of the river Arve and now the other (depending on the whim of the town council), formerly encircled by railings and a ring of stone, today blending democratically into the surroundings of the Post Office, but always and forever turning towards Mont Blanc, the mountain they had conquered in days long gone, Balmat pointing a confident forefinger in its direction, Saussure contemplating it with the resolute gaze of a man determined to overcome all obstacles ... during the hundred years they had stood there, they had often felt quite overcome by despair. What on earth had made the French, Swiss, Italian and English Alpine Clubs, the Appalachian Mountain Club of Boston, the Society of Austrian Tourists and the Academy of Science decide, in 1887, to erect a monument passing sentence of forced immobility on two men who had so loved, so dearly loved striding out vigorously over the rugged mountains around Chamonix a century earlier?

Nor was this stationary existence the least of their woes. It was very cruel, too, to be exposed to such stupid remarks.

'Hey, you seen those weird guys?'

'Cor, not what you'd call the Venus of Milo!'

'Why'd they want to put a statue of Christopher Columbus discovering America up here?'

'Dad! Dad, look at them green men! Are they Martians?'

Once, just once a lady – admittedly a very, very old lady – had stopped in front of the monument exclaiming, 'Now that's what I call a man!' But they couldn't tell which of them she meant, and the fact that her comment seemed principally intended for the ears of the frail little old gentleman accompanying their admirer deprived it of some force.

As for the mountaineers, they passed by without sparing their bold predecessors a glance of emotion, respect or veneration, taking no more notice of them than if they had been a telephone kiosk or a fire hydrant.

It was certainly very hard to spend a hundred years exposed to the indifference of their fellow mountaineers and the insulting remarks of the general public, and to the elements as well: rain, snow, hoar-frost, periods when it froze, thawed and then froze again, winds, rime, and the chilly little mists that rose from the Arve. Balmat was to some extent protected by the metal hat which did at least shade his eyes, but

Saussure had only his wig, and could think himself lucky if it didn't have a nightcap or an enamel fondue dish popped on top of it by some urchin intending to raise a laugh. For bad weather and sarcastic remarks were as nothing to the constant humiliations inflicted upon them, simply by virtue of their being stuck there defenceless in the middle of Chamonix, a butt for the silliest of jokes.

They had certainly had their enemies, that heroic pair of bronze mountaineers! From the first, there had been no shortage of people who thought it very clever to inflict an assortment of disrespectful graffiti, practical jokes in the worst possible taste, and ridiculous accessories on the conquerors of Mont Blanc. One day they found themselves with inky faces; on another occasion they were made up like a couple of floozies, their lips painted red, their eyelids green and their cheeks mauve. They had pairs of glasses perched on their noses, they had chamber-pots put on their heads, they had bras draped over them. Balmat and his pointing finger seemed particularly stimulating to the imagination. All manner of things had been hung from that finger: a red balloon, a string bag, a fishing rod, a condom, a Chinese lantern. And then there was the Popular Front period of the 1930s, when some bright spark had chopped off the finger so that Balmat was left with nothing but a fist, which he was unfortunately obliged to shake at his beloved Mont Blanc until his finger was replaced. Saussure's hat, lying at his feet on the pedestal, had been stolen. So had the stock Balmat held in his left hand. And so had the rest of their gear: the bag, the thermometer, the geologist's hammer, all the bronze items scattered around their feet. They were replaced a little later, arranged in a different way, no one knows why. Nor was that all! There was the time when practical jokers gave them a trail of white footprints, coming down from the pedestal to the asphalt of the road, turning right towards the Place de l'Église, making for the junction with the rue Vallot and then on into the rue de l'Hôtel-de-Ville, ending at the top of the little flight of steps with the notice saying *Public Toilet* above it. A nice pair of Charlies they looked next day! All Chamonix had come along to see the sight, laughing, taking note of the way the trail went, and jeering at the glorious heroes.

'Needed a piss after all that time, eh, mates?'

And all these insults had to be borne impassively, in silence.

It was over the last few years, however, that life had become really unbearable, with the entrance upon the scene of a ghastly layabout who answered to the name of Eustache Lenoble, better known by his nickname of Nono. Nono was truly possessed by the spirit of evil. He it was who regularly threw café chairs, dustbins from riverside houses, and supermarket trolleys into the Arve. He it was who smashed shop windows and tore telephones out of public kiosks. He it was who stole skis if their owners took their eyes off their property for a split second. He it was who emptied parked cars of their contents. And he it was who lifted sleeping bags, mountaineering equipment and money from campers' tents. It was Nono, again, who went up to Alpine huts to pinch ice-axes and boots before the mountaineers woke. And all this for nothing but the simple pleasure of doing harm, since most of the stolen items ended up in crevasses or mountain streams. Finally, it was Nono who smeared soap or worse-smelling substances over the rock of Les Gaillands before the guides did their climbing demonstration; it was Nono who started fires and caused bomb scares. In short, Nono was a thoroughly ugly customer. But his number one victims, his favourite targets, were the unfortunate Saussure and Balmat. They were at the end of their tether. Sometimes he would pelt them with ripe tomatoes or smother them in shaving cream when he got back from his nefarious nocturnal expeditions. Sometimes he would pour honey over them, just to act as glue for the white feathers which he then applied. Sometimes he put Frankenstein or Elephant Man masks on their faces. All his pranks, indeed, were unpleasant, humiliating and distressing. In addition, Nono was as slippery as an eel: the police had never been able to lay hands on him, and he did so much damage that public opinion in the valley thought an entire gang must be at work.

But what could poor Saussure and Balmat do? The world of statues operates by an ethical system which consists of remaining impassive, saying nothing, and never moving an inch while any living soul might possibly be watching. Statues in museums are lucky: when night comes they can yawn, stretch, crack their wooden, bronze or marble joints and exchange the latest gossip. Statues in public places have no such liberty. Just sometimes, on dark November nights when the fog was particularly thick, when the casino had closed its doors, when the people of Chamonix and even Nono were asleep – just sometimes, on the stroke of three in the morning, Saussure and Balmat would venture to take a little walk as far as the War Memorial with the statue of the French Soldier of the First World War on it, to have a chat with someone else for a change. But the Old Contemptible, lost as he was in nostalgic contemplation, wasn't very entertaining company. Once he had told you all about 'his' war he went back to his silent meditations, slung around with all his kit of ammunition pouches and mess tins, his rifle pointing skyward, and emerged from thought only to raise the stick in his left hand and the laurel wreath in his right hand from time to time, announcing that he was going 'over the top'. The fact was that when you'd heard about his war a dozen times or more, the story became rather boring. However, he was the only person they could possibly visit in the entire town of Chamonix, and even so they had to take risks to talk to him. Then the two mountaineers would make their way stealthily back, crossing the Avenue Michel-Croz in a fever of anxiety, going along the bank of the Arve and taking up their eternal watch again, full of palpitations after their adventure.

One day, however, something new happened. An official visit to Chamonix was imminent, and a commission went round the town with a view to making arrangements. The experts stopped briefly in front of the statue of Saussure and Balmat.

'Those two need cleaning,' someone said. 'There are stains on them, and places where the verdigris has run. It looks bad!'

'Then the French Soldier had better be cleaned too while we're about it,' added someone else.

'Find some specialist outfit to do the job,' the first speaker told a secretary who was taking notes.

And the group moved away, leaving Saussure and Balmat feeling very pleased with the prospect of renovation. Their pleasure did not last long. A dreaded shape appeared round the corner of the Monchu restaurant. It was Nono, following the experts at a distance and no doubt anticipating ways to disrupt the plans. Every time they set eyes on Nono, fear, revulsion and impotence made their bronze blood boil. Nono was recognizable a long way off. He was a puny little creature; you'd never suspect his strength. His low forehead, hidden by a long, greasy fringe, contrasted with the shaven back of his head. He had a scowl, a snub nose, sly, thin lips, and he wore leather clothing and walked with a swagger in an attempt to make himself look jaunty. Furtively inspecting the vicinity, he contented himself for once with directing a jet of saliva towards the monument, but he was back next night to pour motor oil over it. In dismay, Saussure and Balmat wondered how he would react to their forthcoming restoration.

Unaware of such threats, the commission had continued its work. One grey late October day, two council workmen came to erect a high fence round Saussure and Balmat, and round the French Soldier too. The renovation work was to be carried out behind this palisade.

'Step on it!' one workman told the other. 'We've got to get this lot up by tonight!'

'We'll get it up okay,' replied his companion. 'What's the flap in aid of? Anyway, I can tell you, I've seen the schedule, and the cleaning's not due to start till after All Saints' Day. That's Wednesday, and this is only Friday, right? So what's the hurry? They'll be stuck here behind these planks for five whole days, waiting to be scrubbed down. Five days, what a bore, poor old things! Hard cheese, mates!'

And indeed, the two statues discovered that they were now walled up in a tall and impenetrable little fort, without so much as the chance of admiring a sunset over Mont Blanc.

'Well, 'pon my soul, Monsieur de Saussure,' groaned Balmat, as night fell, 'this bain't no joke! We be in quod now, that's for sure! Ah, I do miss them mountains! I'd give t' world to be back on Montanvert, I would! Just the once, just a' breathin' in of t' good air up there. Do ye remember 'un, sir?'

'Remember it? Do I not, Balmat, my good fellow!' sighed Saussure. 'Ah, do I not, indeed! Pray rest assured, I too would give the World to ...But stay! An Idea presents itself to my Imaginative Faculties! Balmat, my good man – within the Space of four Days, is it not conceivable that we might once more ascend Mont Blanc as we did in days of Yore? For such is the Span of time at our Command! Thus concealed behind this wooden Rampart, we might vanish hence as if into Thin Air, our Absence marked by none. Departing once the Shades of Night have fallen, we might set forth on our Way at three of the Clock, and return hither to Chamouny before our Scouring is to commence. Ah, could we but climb Mont Blanc once more, that same Ascent we made two centuries since, how vastly it would Gratify my Soul!'

'Bless me, Monsieur de Saussure!' stammered Balmat. 'Who but ye 'ud ever get suchlike notions, sir? Blow me if I don't see we there a'ready! We be to set out tonight, do 'ee say, sir?'

'Aye, to be sure, when all the Rustic Folk are wrap't in Slumber. We would gain the Summit of the Montagne de la Côte, whereon we might pass the second night, to continue on our way up the Glaciers the day thereafter, taking our Repose in some Cavern in the Snows near the Grand Plateau, as on our first Ascent. And the next day – ah, can it be? My heart near fails me, merely at the Thought! The next day we would attain the very Peak of Mont Blanc! Once situated thereon, I would undertake certain Scientifick Observations which I had not the Leisure to pursue on the Occasion of our Previous Climb. To that end, we would convey with us those Instruments of the Physickal Sciences which the Sculptor has been so thoughtful as to leave disposed about our Feet. We would then commence our Descent, with a view to passing the next Night sheltered by the Rocks of the Grands Mulets. Thereafter, on the day following, we would return to the Priory Lands of Chamouny and their bosky Glades, hiding therein until the propitious Shades of Night should once more fall, those Shades being well designed to allow us to escape Observation in the regaining of our Pedestal. In consequence, we would be back at our Post here on the night between Tuesday and Wednesday, some hours before they embark upon the Labour of Scouring. 'Tis too Excellent an Opportunity to be forfeited! God alone knows if another such will ever fall to our Lot!'

'Ye're right there, Monsieur de Saussure! Sure as I be from Les Pélerins, we 'as to take us chance. An' as for t' route, I knows it by 'eart, that be a fact. I been up t' mountain nineteen times afore this, t' third time wi' your good self, sir. Why, I could 'a climbed 'un blindfold. Shake 'ands on it, sir, I'm your man!'

'Then we are both of One Mind, my dear Balmat! But would it not be amiable in us to inform the French Soldier of our Plan? Who knows whether he might not care to join us? Furthermore, he would reinforce the Strength of our Party! On our first Expedition, as you will doubtless recollect, we had with us eighteen Guides and a Domestic Servant. To be Three, rather than but Two alone, must surely be advantageous. Let us call upon him once the Streets are empty.'

And so they did. A little later, moving several planks aside, Saussure and Balmat slipped out of their shelter and, under cover of a useful little mist just rolling into the valley, reached the square where the War Memorial stood and entered the enclosure surrounding the gallant infantryman, all without a hitch.

'Halloa there, Soldier!' said Balmat. 'We be off to climb Mont Blanc, we be. Do 'ee care to come along o' we?'

'No!' replied the French Soldier, very military and succinct.

'Allow me to Persuade you otherwise, my good Friend,' said Saussure. 'I believe you have not Sufficiently Pondered the reasons for your decision. For an Unique Opportunity offers itself to us! Thanks to the wooden Lattens which at this Present conceal us from the world, not a

Mortal Soul will mark our Absence. And we have Certain Knowledge that the Scouring to which we are to be subjected will not commence until Wednesday next.'

'Pack it in!' replied the Soldier. 'Us lads up at the front in the trenches, we ain't applying for leave right, left and centre! Anyways, who'd I apply *to*? Ho yus, I can just see the Military College Commandant's face if I barge in asking him to sign me chitty!'

'Why, man, ye bain't got no call to ask leave o' no one!' said Balmat. 'Just come along o' we, why don't 'ee?'

'Nothing doing!' said the French Soldier. 'Asides, I'm busy getting ready for Remembrance Day.'

'But there bain't nowt for 'ee to do on Remembrance Day! Nowt in t' world!' said the astonished Balmat.

'What d'you mean, nowt?' asked the old hero indignantly. 'You're dead wrong there, mate! I got to concentrate, see? I got to keep my bearing correct, I got to look modest and martial both at once – that takes practice, right? I got to check up on my position and keep my glance steady … It's only a fortnight off. Lord knows if I'll be ready in time! So put a sock in it!'

'Very good, very good!' said Saussure. 'Prithee, do not Agitate yourself, my good fellow. I am Persuaded we shall do very well without you. Farewell, and now permit us to Retire.'

'We'll be seein' 'ee soon,' added Balmat.

'Cheers!' replied the French Soldier, obligingly enough.

But when the two men had moved away, he muttered to himself: 'Climb Mont Blanc! Skiving off! No sentry on duty ever leaves his post, for a start. Asking me to desert, no less! Me, desert! Who'd credit it? There's civilians for you!'

Meanwhile, Balmat and Saussure had reached their pedestal again and were preparing for their great adventure, gathering up the equipment scattered around them.

'It be a cryin' shame they never give me more rope about my middle!' sighed Balmat. 'Aye, well, we be bound to make do with what we got!'

At dead of night, when the clock on the tower of St Michael's Church struck three, the two statues silently left their post, carefully readjusting the planks they had moved to let themselves out. Muffling the sound of their bronze footsteps, they set off through Chamonix, walking down the Rue du Lyret. No one heard them. There were no lights in the windows of any of the houses. The people of Chamonix were asleep, and none of them, either that morning or during the days that followed, had the faintest idea that the bronze mountaineers had taken their strange departure.

But taken it they certainly had! After walking for some minutes Saussure and Balmat skirted the Aiguille du Midi téléphérique station, which they scrutinized with curiosity, and found themselves on the Route Blanche.

'Eh, see what a fine road they'm built we!' marvelled Balmat. 'See the width of 'un! Whatever 'ud my old grandad 'a said, if'n 'e could 'a drove his mules down a road like this 'ere!'

'Let us continue Earnestly in our endeavours to take every Precaution, my Friend,' advised Saussure. 'Should one of their Carriages pass by, we must be ready to Cast Ourselves full length in the Ditch the moment we observe its Lanterns.'

'Ah, never ye fret, sir!' replied Balmat. 'Why, 'tis but a league to Les Bossons, then it be an hour's walk to the mountain, and after that we bain't like to meet a soul. It be out of season, ye'll mind! Happen we'll 'ave t' mountain all to usselves!'

And indeed, they crossed the valley without any problems. They did not make much speed at first, to be sure, since it was hard to get their joints and muscles moving again, stiff as they were from such a long period of inactivity, but gradually their bodies loosened up and their metal limbs became flexible once more.

Eventually the mountaineers reached the last chalets of the Mont des Bossons, huddled on the mountain shelf, closed and deserted this cold night in late autumn. Without the throngs of tourists who apparently liked only the over-crowding of the high season, the valley returned to its profound, pastoral calm. The two men climbed up along an Alpine meadow of frosted willow-herb above the hamlet; the milky clarity of the mist allowed them to guess at fluffy white tufts, congealed and stiffened by frost and humidity, on the dry stems of the plants. And yet, in spite of the night and the season of the year, they could sense the life of the mountain. An animal moved somewhere in the cover of the woods; a leaf fell to the ground with a dry rustle.

'Ah, Monsieur de Saussure!' marvelled Balmat. 'Such a scent as there be in t' air! Bless me if 'un don't still smell of t' 'ay and t' flowers! A man can breathe easy up 'ere! 'Twere a fine idea as ye 'ad, sir!'

Reaching the undergrowth, they climbed a little farther to get past the mountain hut of the Bossons Glacier. Then, feeling weary, they finally stopped a little to one side of the path in the middle of the forest, letting themselves fall on a thick carpet of moss. Draping the bronze folds of the blanket which Saussure carried over his shoulder around them, they sank into the delightful depths of a healing sleep.

Daybreak surprised them there. Birds had been singing for some time when they woke, surrounded by the beauties of autumn. Spruce trees grew here and there, their dark shapes setting off the greeny golds, yellow golds, russet golds and tawny golds which made the forest glow as if with some internal light. Above them arched the brightly bedizened branches of a birch, its light leaves trembling like copper sequins. Elsewhere, larches spread their scarlet plumes in the air, in a wild blaze of colour. A thin mist lingered in the undergrowth. The air itself had a pleasant, fresh smell of moss and mushrooms, and looking through the trees you could see that farther down the valley the day had not yet thawed the white frost that coated the grass with a silver halo.

Silent, amazed and delighted, the two men held their breath. They had forgotten how beautiful it was!

At last, Saussure spoke.

'Observe, my dear Jacques,' said he, 'observe how Strangely and Marvellously the Supreme Being hath perfected His Creation! See how the renewal essential to Life is Garbed in Grace and Splendour, ere Boreas bring wintry Snows to lay a shelt'ring Mantle o'er the Forests. Contemplating God in all His Works, in spirit I approach th' Eternal Light. Yea, its Brightness dazzles mine Eyes! The Admirable Picture here presented by the Genius of Nature reveals it fully: all is Harmony and Fair Proportion, while Man alone offers a Spectacle of Chaos and Disorder.'

'An' that's a fact. Ye've only got to look at Nono,' sighed Balmat.

'Aye, my Friend, 'tis very true, in faith, that we have undergone many Outrages at the Hands of Men, but now we are granted the Boon of Escaping them for a few brief days. Let us enjoy these Sublime Moments bestowed upon us by Fate, and Nurture no Vain Regrets. Let us proceed, in all Serenity of Mind, towards that icy Colossus which our Feet will soon press once more. Let us forget past Torments, contemplating only Present Felicity. The Weather bids Fair! All seems to promise a Fortunate Conclusion.'

'Aye, it do be very pleasant,' agreed Balmat. 'I slept like a log, meself, and now I be fresh as a daisy! Why, it do the 'eart good just to see them pretty autumn colours! That little mist do say it be a fine day a-comin', too. Chances are we'll be a mite cold up top, but I do swear we be well able to climb that gurt white mole'ill!'

It was a delightful day. In point of fact, they did not go very far. Keeping in the undergrowth so as to avoid anyone who might be out walking, the two mountaineers kept admiring the spectacle presented to them by Nature: russet leaves crunching underfoot, big burdocks flecked with brown by the frost, the brightness of golden rowans, their scarlet berries standing out against the flying vapours of the mist, the play of light and clouds, now concealing and now revealing a landscape which sometimes seemed to be dissolving, as if unreal in its spectral lightness, and the next moment was blazing with life in a glorious wealth of shapes and colours. Suddenly Chamonix came into sight below them, at the bottom of a great chasm.

'Bless me, do 'ee see the size o' it!' said Balmat. 'Who'd ever 'a thought it? 'Pon my soul, they been a-buildin' all over – where t' avalanches might come down an' all! Tell 'ee what, sir, I bain't surprised us don't see so many cattle in t' streets nowadays. Why, there bain't a mite o' pasture left for t' grazin'!'

'The Way of the World is to change, my Friend, and Man's Industry knows no bounds. Yet one may Easily Perceive that the old Simplicity and Purity of the people of these Valleys and their customs are greatly Altered thereby. I am All Aflame with Eagerness to ascend higher, that I may at Last set eyes upon my dear City of Geneva. No doubt Geneva too will be much Transformed!'

Closer to the mountain, the clouds became increasingly tenuous, and the growing luminosity suggested that the sun was not far off. Soon the mountaineers found themselves level with the Les Pyramides chalet, above the frozen chaos of the Bossons Glacier, a cosmic shattering of sharp points, blades and gulfs with the gnarled shapes of a few twisted trees standing out in front of it.

'My Friend,' said Saussure, 'see ye yon Arolla Pines which might appear to totter vertiginously above the Abrupt and Steely Blue of the Precipice? I am reminded of the curious Oriental Wash Drawings brought back from China by a Traveller friend of mine who – '

'Begging your pardon, Monsieur de Saussure,' interrupted Balmat, 'but sure as I be a man o' Savoie, ye says that very same thing to I in this same place two centuries gone! Happen 'un bain't just t' same trees, but 'un looks mighty like. And ye says to I then, ye says – '

'Well and Good, well and Good! I beg *your* Pardon, I am sure!' put in

Saussure, somewhat irritated. 'A man may chance to Repeat himself, I suppose; no doubt it comes of Advancing Age. And I trust you will Grant me it is not easy to remember Perfectly, in every Point, those Words one may have uttered two hundred years previously. However, I am glad to find that you still recall my Instructive Remarks, even if you may consider that I am Rambling Somewhat.'

'There now, Monsieur de Saussure, never ye fret! I on'y spoke in passing, like! On account o' the coincidence. An' I be sure ye don't ramble much, not yet. Not for a man o' your age, nay, niver!'

A sudden wind rose and interrupted this discussion, blowing away the last of the mist veiling the mountain. Suddenly, appearing to float in the clear blue of the sky, the grey ridges of the Aiguillette and Brévent were revealed, emerging from their cloudy fleece, and then, soon afterwards, both very near and infinitely far away, the Aiguille du Midi and Mont Blanc du Tacul in all the immensity of their slopes and their snows, the dazzle of their whiteness, the radiant lightness of the altitude. There was absolutely nothing for it but to respond to their call. In spite of the sun, the cold was biting, and soon the short grass, the browned rhododendrons and the path itself were covered with a thin layer of the first snow. However, it was still easy to walk along the path, which had been improved over the course of time.

'Mercy on us, 'un be quite a 'ighway!' marvelled Balmat. 'Look at 'un, will 'ee? A man could take a 'orse down this 'ere path. And when it do go up steep-like, they'm put marks o' yallery paint so's a man can find t' way! Well, dang me, who'd 'a credited 'un! See where they'm writ "Danger" to send 'ee right, not left? Ah, they be timid folk nowadays – bain't no vartue left in t' climbing at all! Happen 'un 'ad been so in our days, 'twould a' been a deal easier!'

They rounded Mont Corbeau and continued to climb, as if walking a road in mid-air. Sometimes the silence was broken by the sound of a stone rolling into the abyss, sometimes by a cataclysmic crash as a number of séracs fell on a glacier, or by the dull rumble of the mountain in labour. They were beginning to feel the effects of the altitude, and the exertions of the last twenty-four hours were tiring to muscles unused to such effort. But once the mountaineers reached the top of the rocky slope and came to the Junction, where the soil ends and the universe of ice begins, they were amply rewarded for their pains. The world where they had arrived had nothing in common with the world of the valleys. Before them, in a fantastic foreshortened view, spread the great vista of high mountains dominated by the Aiguille and the Dôme du Goûter, Mont Blanc du Tacul and Mont Maudit, with scraps of ragged cloud flying fast behind them.

'Not too wore out, be 'ee, sir?' asked Balmat solicitously. 'It be a while since I heard 'ee say aught! Short o' breath, eh? But we be up now, an' if so be as ye feel breathless, 'twill pass off wi' a good night's rest. Eh, 'tis a shame that wooden hut ye built 'ere be gone. We'll be obliged to shelter in what folks call Balmat's Den now. But we'll be snug enough in there – tired as we be, we'll sleep like babbies, and tomorrow, I warrant 'ee, we'll be fresh as a one-year old chamois for t' mountain. Ah, she be a beauty! So be easy, sir, and see the view we got up 'ere, with the light a-fadin' and the Good Lord sendin' we a fine pink sunset. 'Pon my soul, a statue don't live to see many sichlike days! I be partly minded to pass t' night out o' doors, eyes open for to see me fill o' t' stars and t' moon in that fine gurt sky.'

Wisely, however, the two mountaineers gave themselves up to refreshing sleep when night fell, and they were well rested when they set out to cross the Junction next day. Joined by the bronze rope, and using two long sticks providently cut by Balmat in the forest farther down the mountain, they set out through the maze of crevasses, caves and frozen crests which separated them from the Grands Mulets. The season had been dry, and the snow had not yet filled up cavities, formed bridges or smoothed passages. They were constantly obliged to tack about, take winding ways, climb up or down and retrace their steps, and in this meandering manner they made their way through the vast, frozen labyrinth.

'Such a vast Quantity of Ice!' sighed Saussure. 'These sharp Crests, these Vertiginous Precipices! We have in excess of six thousand feet yet to climb, and already methinks the Air grows thinner. Great God, into what Manner of Venture have we cast ourselves? Are we still of an Age for such Audacity? Shall we ever emerge from this Labyrinth, which appears as it had been Fashioned by the Hands of Titans? How can I now traverse this Steep and Dangerous Rising Way, with the Bottomless Abyss on either side?'

'Do 'ee just keep a-goin', sir!' Balmat told him. 'Do 'ee watch the notches I be about to make, an' plant your feet in 'em well. 'Tis lucky we be wearing these 'ere bronze shoes – happen they'll give we a bit o' purchase on t' ice, for there bain't much thick snow up top. Watch out now, sir! It be a mite tricky just here! There – do 'ee catch hold o' my stick! 'Old on, now! Don't 'ee be too proud to 'aul on 'un a bit! Take 'un easy – there, ye be over! Now, what be next? Hm ... well, don't 'ee budge from 'ere, sir, I be a-goin' to look ...'

Crossing the Junction took the mountaineers a long, long time, but they finally reached the other side of the labyrinth, and stopped to recover their strength at the foot of the Grands Mulets, seizing the opportunity to marvel at the huge metal hut anchored to the first of the peaks, such an improvement on the wooden hut Saussure had caused to be built in 1787 in the same place, on the higher rocks.

'Well, we bain't there yet!' observed Balmat after a brief rest. 'Off we goes, sir! Do 'ee know 'ow much farther it be if'n we be to reach t' Grand Plateau this 'ere evening?'

'Nigh on three thousand Feet!' sighed Saussure.

' 'Ere we do go, then! Time we was pickin' up us gear an' movin' on. This be a gurt long climb, long and tedious. So seein' as we be bound to tackle 'un, no dilly-dallyin'! Off we do go, sir – best foot forrard!'

Although the way up the slopes that followed was less tortuous, it was indeed long and steep. Sometimes a huge crevasse forced the mountaineers to go a long way round, adding to the distance they had to travel. Their imposing stature and the solidity of their constitution were certainly an advantage, but on the other hand there was the inconvenience of having to raise such a great weight of bronze from the ground with every step they took. For hours, they climbed on along the coomb leading to the Grand Plateau, dazzled by the reflection of sun on snow. Saussure was already experiencing some difficulty in breathing, and stopped every hundred paces to get his breath back and take a brief rest.

'Bain't gettin' no younger, sir, be ye?' remarked Balmat. ' 'Ere, let me have them confounded Scientifick Instruments ye be luggin' along of 'ee, do! What a daft notion to take into yer head, lumberin' yerself wi' that lot! Science be a very fine thing, for sure, but ye still has to move, sir, and speaking for meself, I'd sooner 'a brought a ladder. Fair bit o' time a ladder would 'a saved we! But I knows 'ee, sir, and I knows it bain't no manner o' good, ye won't shift wi'out such stuff! There, now! Ye'll be lighter that way, and I'd sooner not delay gettin' to t' Petit Plateau, on account o' they séracs up there.'

The layer of fresh snow was gradually becoming thicker, which made walking no easier. Its surface was partly frozen, forming a crust which sometimes bore up but sometimes gave way under their feet, so that making any progress was an exhausting business. Under these new conditions, the two men initially tried to take turn and turn about in the lead, but Saussure lacked Balmat's powerful vigour and managed by dint of tenacity rather than strength when it was his turn to go in front. The effort of forging a path through the deep snow exhausted him, and he took a very long time about it. At one point, he was so weary that he failed to sound out the ground ahead of him, and suddenly dropped into a crevasse, both legs down, holding himself up only with difficulty by his outstretched arms and stick. Once he was out again, Balmat took over the lead as by right.

'Saints above, this be tough going!' he grunted, letting off steam. 'Pity that there Soldier wouldn' come. 'Twouldn't be amiss to 'ave two men takin' turns beatin' a path through sichlike deep snow – but there we be, an' I tell 'ee summat, sir, 'tis a right shame the folks of Chamonix, or all they Alpine Clubs or whatsomever they do go callin' 'emselves these days, didn't never put up no statue to good old Doctor Paccard!* 'Twere 'im as found this route, warn't it? Even if that Monsieur Bourrit done 'is best to make I say different, arterwards. Well, I be real glad to give 'im the credit today! Oh, aye, 'twere Monsieur Paccard what made the first ascent with me! Fact of the matter be, if I 'adn't 'a put on a spurt at t' last, 'e'd 'a reached the summit alone. And 'twere thanks to 'im I never give up lower down, too. T' conquest o' Mont Blanc, why, it were Paccard's more than yourn or mine, sir – there's human ingratitude for ye, eh? And if they'd on'y 'a put up a statue to 'im too, ye may be sure 'e'd 'a gone along o' we an' not come over all pernickety like that there Soldier! Well, there it be, ye can't remake the world to yer likin'. So do 'ee keep a-goin', Monsieur de Saussure! Come on, it bain't so bad along 'ere. Won't never do to slacken t' pace now. How far do 'ee reckon we still 'as to go?'

'About nine hundred feet to the Grand Plateau, and some two thousand seven hundred more to be climbed tomorrow. It is now three quarters past four of the Clock in the Afternoon. The Barometer stands at eighteen inches and two lines, while the Thermometer displays a Temperature of two point five degrees above Freezing,' replied Saussure, who had always been passionately fond of precise scientific observation.

* This story was written before the City of Chamonix launched an appeal for funds for a statue of Paccard, to celebrate the bicentenary in 1986 of the first ascent of Mont Blanc, an idea that originated in the present work.

'Fancy!' remarked Balmat politely. 'Bain't cold enough, then? And there's summat else as do trouble me – t' ill-weather cloud atop of Mont Blanc and they veils, like, up in t' sky, they don't look good to I. There was red clouds in t' morning too, and like the country folk hereabouts do say: "Red sky in t' morning, shepherd's warning." 'Tis to be 'oped we bain't obliged to face a storm.'

By the time they reached the Grand Plateau, the sky was entirely grey. At these altitudes there were no good bivouac sites, so Balmat used the geologist's hammer to excavate a kind of hollow in a dip in the ground, and the two men half buried themselves in it. A boisterous wind had risen as night fell, and soon the peaks were being devastated by storm-clouds and a hurricane. Violent gusts swept the mountainside, and at times the mountaineers had to brace themselves against their equipment, to keep both it and themselves from being carried away like straws in the wind. The air was filled with electricity, and a sudden flash of lightning shot through the night.

'What a Singular and Prodigious Drama it is,' remarked Saussure, 'to find oneself at such an Elevation, imprisoned in a Body of Metal, and facing the Unleashed Fury of the Thunderbolts! Prithee note: we are all covered with Flames! Let us hope we be not struck by Lightning! I could not then answer for the Happy Issue of our Venture, for I entertain the Liveliest Premonition that the Outcome would not be a Fortunate one. It seems as though these Dreadful Thunderclaps were multiplied an Thousandfold by the Echoes of the Mountains, shaking them to their Very Foundations. The Lightning Flashes dazzle me. God grant this Storm may swiftly Abate! It should not be of long duration at this Season of the Year.'

Sure enough, the storm did gradually die down, but it was followed by fog and then by snow. When a pale dawn finally cast light on the scene, the entire landscape was shrouded in thick mist. Only a few paces away, nothing at all was visible, and grey vapour rose between the statues themselves, blurring their outlines. It was impossible to climb on, and no doubt impossible to climb down too.

'Well, we'll have to make t' best of it,' said Balmat. 'We mun just wait where we be! 'Tain't the best o' places, I'll allow, but it be safer than setting out Gawd knows where. We can't even think o' findin' us way through all this 'ere cloud – why, ye could cut it wi' a knife. So 'ere we stays! If so be as it do lift, we can go on, and if it don't, well, let we think o' that tomorrow morning.'

The day passed without any change in the weather. It was still cold and foggy, and snow fell now and then. Evening came, and a long November night began. This was the fourth time they had made camp. Saussure was suffering a good deal from the discomfort.

'Ah, my Friend,' he groaned, 'what is to become of us, left without Shelter or Aid? I am unaccustomed to such Inconveniences, and the Inclemency of the Weather, as it appears to me, gives us Strong Grounds for discouragement. Shall we ever see the end of this Dreadful Night? Will Glorious Day ever peep again? I am tormented by an Infinite Number of Evils, and cannot Compose myself to Slumber. My Breeches adhere to the Ice. My Heart seems to beat but feebly. These Gelid Temperatures are terrible! I fear I am Expiring!'

'Nay, niver say that, sir!' protested Balmat. 'This bain't no feather bed, to be sure, and what wi' t' snow, and t' black north wind – dang me, we ain't got so much as mittens to wear! Me own blood's a-freezin' too. We mun pray this 'ere curst weather don't last too long and I do fancy it bain't snowing so 'ard now. We be bound to 'old out, sir. 'Uddle up to me and keep close.'

The storm ended around the middle of the night, and the sky gradually cleared. The glacial basin shone in the moonlight, but the cold was sharper than ever. Dawn found the mountaineers very stiff. Saussure shook Balmat, who had fallen asleep.

'Awaken, Jacques, my good fellow! Fine Weather and daylight have delivered us from our Perilous Situation, and the Colossus of the Alps should offer us no Further Defiance. To tell Truth, I know not how I shall be able to walk, but it fills me with Courage and hope to see our Design so near Fulfilment.'

'We be stiff now, stiff and poorly! We can't put one foot in front of 'tother afore we warms up. We mun stir our stumps – get usselves moving, loosen up again. One! Two! Do like I, sir!'

After a vigorous session of gymnastics, the mountaineers had recovered most of their strength, and felt full of energy and the determination to reach their goal. Conversations overheard from time to time in Chamonix had led them to understand that there was a new way along the ridge now, but they did not intend to try it. That route had seemed too steep in 1784, and there was no reason to suppose that its inclination had changed since. They therefore went left, towards the *Ancien Passage*, and reached the rising slope between the Rochers Rouges. A layer of fresh snow covered the ice here, making the ascent particularly difficult and dangerous, but the mountaineers, carefully carving out white steps on the mountainside, eventually vanquished this obstacle. The summit still seemed far away. They were stopping every fifteen paces or so now to get their breath back, and not making such good progress as they had hoped.

'Well, fancy,' said Balmat, 'just fancy: I just took a route as they forbade the Chamonix guides to go in 1866! Ye can see why, at that. In a blue funk, I was! Yet I dunno no other way back down. We oughter pay more heed to what they tourists says while they're a-gawpin' round our pedestal. I be fair wore out! I reckon as 'ee be wore out too, sir!'

'I am incommoded by the Dazzle,' explained Saussure. 'Also by Breathlessness, Nausea, and Palpitations of the Heart.'

'Dang me, that won't do!' said Balmat in alarm.

'Wait, wait! I had not yet concluded. My Strength fails me, and I feel I shall Swoon at any moment. But I am most Infallibly Determined to continue to the End!'

'Ah, spoken like yerself, sir!' replied Balmat. 'When I sees ye so, why, I tells meself as ye ain't changed a bit! Dogged as ever! Ye might be from Chamonix yerself, so ye might! 'Ere we do go, then. On'y three 'unnerd feet or so now!'

'Four hundred or More, I fear, since we have not yet reached the Petits Mulets. But get there we will!'

And get there they did! A little later, they were expressing their joy on the summit they had longed so much to reach. The bright Alps stretched below them as far as the eye could see, separated by valleys blue with mist. The vast horizon seemed lost in infinity. Saluting one another fraternally, the two men embraced with emotion and a sonorous metallic clang.

'Sublime and Dizzying Panorama!' said Saussure. 'How great is Nature as she left the Creator's Hands! Here we may indeed contemplate the most Singular and Ravishing of sights. Mark those Awesome Slopes, those Amazing Gulfs, those Precipices dropping sheer, more than ten thousand feet! Admire that Horizon, its Mists allowing us to divine the presence of the beautiful Lake below. I can scarce believe mine Eyes. 'Tis like a Dream that I may once more admire those Majestick Peaks and formidable Needles, intermingled with Ice and Rock! Did ever you see a View more Magnificent and Imposing than this summit, enveloped in a snowy Cloak whose white Hue merges with that of the Clouds? Than these Great Giants whose Prodigious Heights now lie beneath our feet? How lively is the Satisfaction I feel! Here, in this Abode of Cold and Silence, all seems devised to stamp the sweetest of Emotions upon the Soul.'

'Danged fine sight,' agreed Balmat.

'I take Infinite Pleasure in the accomplishment of our Design,' continued Saussure, 'and I will now proceed to perform certain Physickal Experiments, the height of 14,566 feet 8 inches to which we have ascended being singularly Propitious thereto.'

'Ye certainly don't want to 'ave 'auled all this stuff up 'ere for nowt!' grunted Balmat. 'But make 'aste, sir, do, for when 'ee be done we mun get down this mountain faster than ever we come up. The snow's lost we a day, and even if'n we do travel by night, we'll only just be back in time! So don't ye linger long, sir!'

In fact the weather soon cut short Saussure's experiments. A north-west wind was blowing, raising powdery flakes from the snow and whipping it into the faces of the two statues, who were already white with rime. Saussure and Balmat were obliged to turn back, and as they took one last look at the Alps from the peak it was very unlikely they could ever climb again, emotion brought small bronze tears to the corners of their eyes, where they were instantly frozen by the cold.

'Come, my friend,' said Saussure. 'Nature never made Man or even Statues for these Elevated Regions.'

'Aye, we mun get back! Ready? Off we goes, then!'

The *Ancien Passage* proved even more dangerous than on the way up, and it was a miracle that no avalanche carried the two mountaineers away.

'Not on yer arse, Monsieur de Saussure, saving your honour!' said Balmat, indignantly. 'Not on yer arse! Aye, what a fellow 'un be! Still t' same! Won't ye never learn to keep yer weight forrard coming down'ill, sir? Two 'unnerd years and more of mountaineering, and 'e still don't know ye mun stay good and upright if ye bain't to slip.'

Saussure, recollecting with some mortification that he had once had an engraving retouched, regardless of authenticity, to make his bearing appear more dignified, replied impatiently:

'It seems I am not alone in a Tendency to Repeat myself, my good fellow! And *you* reproach *me* with mentioning those Oriental Pictures once more! I suppose that a due respect for Human Liberties will allow a man the right to his own Mode of Propulsion, and I am far from certain that Mine is not as good as Yours, in that it brings the Centre of Gravity closer to the ground. I am sure that a great many Mountaineers have employed it since my time.'

'Ah, never fret, Monsieur de Saussure! I only spoke on account o' they crevasses down there, seeing as if 'ee sets off that way on yer arse, saving your reverence, there be a mighty strong risk as we won't be back for that there scouring. And think what a to-do there'd be then! We bain't got none too much time as it be.'

But Saussure, recovering breath and strength at these lower altitudes, felt a need to vent his feelings.

'Pray be not Alarmed! All, or almost all, has smiled upon us hitherto. Think, rather, of the Wonderful Feat we have again accomplished! How dearly I would like to add a Chapter to my *Travels in the Alps*! I wonder if the excellent Printing Press of Fauche, which published me so Elegantly of Old, still stands in Neuchâtel? I was very well satisfied with its Work.'

'Don't 'ee chatter away so, sir – look where ye puts yer feet instead. Ye near trod into that 'ole, and who'm to say what do lie beneath? We bain't down yet. To think as we come up all this way! What time do 'ee reckon it be?'

'It will soon be four o'clock of the Afternoon.'

'Hm – let I work the time out! Say we'm to be back around 'arf past four o' the clock tonight. Five at t' most. 'Twill be a two-three hours to get back over the Junction. Say three more a-comin' down t' Montagne de la Côte in t' dark. Another hour, goin' a mite faster this time, on to Chamonix. And happen we wants a little rest at t' foot of the Grands Mulets first – nay, ye take my word for it, sir, the faster we goes the better! We'm bound to walk all night anyways!'

Indeed, evening was not far off when they dropped briefly to the ground at the foot of the Grand Mulets before tackling the final ordeal. Sinking down on a tongue of snow where they could lean back against the rock, they were savouring their triumph and their last moments of peace in the Alpine solitude, when the silence was broken by a cry.

'Dang me, what be that?' asked Balmat. 'I could 'a sworn I 'eard a shout! Be there anyone there?'

'Nay, your Ears did not deceive you, Jacques,' replied Saussure. 'I heard the self-same Clamorous Sound. There can be no Doubt about it. And I dare swear it came from just Above us.'

Moving back a little, the two mountaineers saw a light burning in the windows of the mountain hut. Sounds of violence suddenly proceeded from inside it. To avoid detection, they moved swiftly back into the shelter of the slope.

'Gawd 'elp us, this be a fine thing!' groaned Balmat. 'Someone do be up 'ere, at this time o' the year! And we dussn't risk being seen!'

'No, to be sure! You well know the Laws that govern the Destiny of Statues. It is said that some Calamity, I know not what, will befall should one of us ever reveal himself in his Animated State to the eyes of any ordinary Mortal.'

'We mun just wait for nightfall. And we be short of time as 'tis, and there be a moon too ... 'tis danged curst luck, to be sure!'

At this point a gutted mattress sailed through the air above their heads and landed on the snow.

'Gawd!' swore Balmat. 'They be smashing up the 'ut! Hark at that, will 'ee? They be tearin' of everything out up there, and we can't do nowt to stop 'em. We mun keep mum till that be over, whether so be as they leaves or whether so be as they drops off to sleep – and we mun 'ope they doesn't take too long about it. The sun be a-goin' down already.'

'I suspect there is but One Person there,' said Saussure a few moments late, 'for I heard a Deal of noise, but neither Conversation nor Argument. It would seem, rather, that some Lunatick is giving rein to a Destructive Frenzy in the hut.'

Long moments passed. Then the door up above them opened, and a man abruptly emerged.

'Who the devil be he?' grunted Balmat. 'Some poacher, think 'ee, sir?'

But when he heard the man utter a string of oaths in inebriated tones, their echoes ringing back from the mountains, he recognized the voice.

'Landsakes above!' he exclaimed. 'That be Nono!'

It was indeed Nono. He had climbed from the Plan de l'Aiguille to the Grands Mulets for the sole purpose of looting the hut before winter made the way impassable. The fresh snow which had fallen to a height of about three thousand metres had hidden the heavy tracks of the other pair on the mountain. Sure that he was alone, he had methodically set about destroying everything, sacking the dormitory, slitting mattresses, ripping blankets, sawing through benches and bunk beds, breaking china and the caretaker's kit, emptying the beers and other drinks left over from last summer on the floor, and now and then taking a gulp from a bottle of spirits which he had kept for that purpose. He had just come out to proffer insults in advance to those mountaineers who would visit the hut after him, and to tip a basket full of cutlery and utensils which he had been unable to break out of doors. Its contents clanged for quite a long time as they hit the rock.

'Rapscallion!' said Saussure angrily. 'Must his Evil Disposition lead him to injure his Fellow Men even here? Jacques, we must give the Impudent Rascal a severe Lesson, one which will keep him from ever desiring to commit such Misdeeds again. Let us Show ourselves, and as for what may happen next, well, deuce take it! I would happily give the Scoundrel a Thrashing, but I am Persuaded that we might efficaciously appear to him in Silence, no more, without Resorting to such Violence. No doubt the Fear he feels upon seeing us here will lead him to muse upon his Wickedness and, whatever Else may transpire, will induce him to show us more Respect in future.'

'Whatsoever 'ee do say, Monsieur de Saussure. Ye speak the word and I be your man. That be the worst blackguard ever I met!' replied Balmat, choked with indignation. 'But who'd 'a thought as 'e'd wreck they mountain 'uts, atop of all 'e done to we? 'Ark! There 'e be, a-comin' down now. And 'e do look right befuddled too!'

Having achieved his nefarious purpose, Nono was indeed on his way back. It was the twilight hour when the valleys are already drowned in shadow, but the mountains seem to radiate whiteness in the pale light of the moon. Even Nono was impressed by the deep silence, the apparent solitude of his surroundings, and the mysterious immensity of the landscape when, on reaching the foot of the slope, he jumped down on the snow. Suddenly he saw two tall, dark shapes closing in on him. He recognized them at once. In terror, he stared at the two statues which the fitful light of the moon, alternately hidden and revealed by the driving clouds, animated with spectral life as their sightless eyes stared at him. Nono was not brave except when attacking those who were weaker than himself, had no means of defence, or were absent. Terrified by the threat he saw in this apparition, he let out a howl of fear and darted to one side. He lost his footing, slipped on the ice, fell, slithered down a slope and was engulfed in the immense crevasse that gaped a few metres below. It was so deep that from outside you couldn't even hear the sound when his dislocated body fell and was smashed at the bottom.

'So 'elp me Gawd!' said Balmat. 'Staight into that crevasse 'e went! Well, 'e'll be past aid now! Dead as a doornail, and without no absolution neither, what 'e stood in sore need of, that's for sure!'

'Unfortunate Nono!' sighed Saussure. 'Did ever Mortal Man meet so Dismal a Fate? Acquainted, as it would seem, with Naught but Evil all his days, and now, cut down in the Flower of his Youth, passing away after one last Misdeed. May God have mercy on his Soul!'

'If ye say so, Monsieur de Saussure. That Nono was a reet scoundrel, though, and leastways 'e can't do no more 'arm now 'e's a-roastin' in 'ell.'

'Let us not judge. One final Impulse of Contrition may have passed through his mind. For what befalls thereafter, we must trust to God's Wisdom and Infinite Mercy.'

'Aye, 'tis very true, sir, but I'd sooner know 'e was where 'e is now than makin' trouble for us 'ere on earth. 'E won't breed lice nor poison our lives no more. We can rest easy now, with t' memory of a great climb to warm the cockles of our 'earts. But I just 'ad a notion, sir. Time be short and getting shorter, but while we'm about it, why doesn't we go up there, mend matters as best we can, and bolt t' door to keep t' snow out over t' winter?'

'You are in the Right of it, my Friend. I was thinking much the same myself – indeed, I am Persuaded that it is our duty to those who follow us. This Hut may save precious Human Lives! But we must make haste, lest the Vexatious Setback we have suffered prevent our returning to our Post in time!'

Working as fast as they could, then, the two mountaineers tried to repair the damage Nono had done. They put out cigarette ends smouldering in corners, and restored the place to some kind of order, sweeping the debris into heaps and making sure the doors and windows were shut tight.

'Come on, sir, we mun make 'aste now!' implored Balmat. 'I reckon as I can retrace the path we took up over they séracs in this 'ere moonlight, but remember there's a tidy way to go! Do 'ee let me go in front to reconnoitre – and try to 'old yerself correct back there, sir!'

None the less, it was well past midnight when they reached the top of the Montagne de la Côte.

'Quick, sir, quick!' urged Balmat. 'We mun go down as fast as ever we can now! That scoundrel's cost us hours, so 'e 'as! We mun be there afore daybreak, or Gawd knows what'll come of it! There've been one calamity already, a local man a-seeing of we. I don't like to think what might 'appen if'n we bain't back down in time. We mun take every short cut we can – there bain't no choice now – so do 'ee follow me!'

Quickening their pace in spite of their weariness, the mountaineers made haste towards the valley, but the cover of the woods, deepening the shades of night, slowed them down even more, and when they reached the Route Blanche day was already dawning.

At that precise moment Hector Burgondaz, a retired roadmender whose unfortunately bulbous and rubicund nose had earned him a reputation for intemperance which was only half deserved, was walking across the still deserted Place de la Poste. He had never lost the habit of rising early, and this morning he had gone for a little walk round town. On reaching the bridge over the Arve, he went up to the fence surrounding the monument and decided, out of curiosity, to shift one of the planks and take a look at the work site which was shortly to open.

'Gawd help us!' he exclaimed. 'Somebody's nicked Saussure and Balmat!'

Full of the importance his discovery conferred on him, he carefully replaced the plank and determined to go straight to tell the police, the Mayor, and the Chairman of the Friends of Old Chamonix, whom he woke one by one, in a state of high excitement which struck them as rather odd. However, they got up, telephoned each other, and arranged to meet at the scene of the alleged crime.

Meanwhile, Saussure and Balmat were making their way down the Route Blanche, terrified a car or a pedestrian might appear.

'Nobbut another eighth of a league and us'll be there!' pleaded Balmat. 'Faster, sir, I beg you!'

'I am Mortified to be the cause of delaying you,' gasped Saussure, 'but my Limbs seem made of Lead.'

'No, no, sir, that be bronze, not lead! I be ready to drop meself, aching all over, proper done up, worn to a frazzle I be! But 'tis on'y a matter of minutes now. Come on, in 'eaven's name, come on! We can rest as long as ever we likes arterwards!'

Hector and the authorities met outside the fence.

'Take a look at this, then!' said the old man triumphantly, moving the plank aside.

Behind the wooden wall, Saussure and Balmat stood fixed in their eternal posture, turning towards Mont Blanc, the mountain they had conquered in days long gone, Balmat pointing a confident forefinger in its direction, Saussure contemplating it with the resolute gaze of a man determined to overcome all obstacles . . .

'They're mud all over, right up to their chins,' remarked the Mayor. 'I don't remember them being quite that dirty. Scraping down will do them a world of good.' And when Hector had left, swallowing his surprise with some difficulty, he added, 'Old Burgondaz is in a bad way. Tight as an owl at seven a.m.! I ask you! I wouldn't have thought he was that far gone!'

Work on the statues began during the day. Perched on light scaffolding, two workmen washed them down, rinsed them, scraped them, rubbed them, brushed and polished them.

'That's funny!' said one of them. 'Wonder why the sculptor did that? You'd say they had little bronze tears, like, in the corners of their eyes.'

TABLE TALK

It was one of those freezing February days which make you think the winter will never end. Snow had fallen earlier in the week and had turned to nasty yellow slush in the streets. Only a thin frozen crust remained on the trees, the sills of the balconies and the roofs where occasional icicles had formed. The water in the fountains was frozen. The sky with its low clouds looked opaque and menacing. It was my first year in Paris, and I was homesick for the southern landscape of my birth, its light, even its tramontane wind. I hadn't made many friends yet, and the prospect of this dinner party had quite cheered my week. Brigitte and Étienne were distant cousins of my parents, and I had already been their guest on several occasions. Heaven knows I'd turned up in answer to their first invitation with considerable hesitation and lack of enthusiasm. But I'd been instantly captivated, and now I was really looking forward to the warmth of their welcome, the soft brightness of their rose-coloured sitting room, the crackling of the wood fire in the old-fashioned hearth, the big table with its flowered cloth, and the effusive high spirits of the people gathered round it: a large family, and guests who were always agreeable company. Brigitte knew how to pair off her guests too, and I'd always found myself sitting beside neighbours for whom I felt one of those 'elective affinities' which mean that the conversation isn't just trite, but enters into your real interests. In fact I very much hoped to be next to Marion, like last time.

But when I arrived, full of happy anticipation, I realised that on this particular evening Brigitte's art, strangely, had deserted her. As soon as I came in I felt disappointed. There were far too many people. It was obviously somebody's birthday, and there were extra, makeshift tables scattered about. And when Brigitte, as soon as she had welcomed me, told me about the women I'd be sitting next to, I could feel only a vague antipathy for them.

'Now then, my dear Vincent,' she said. 'Since you know hardly anyone here, I've put you between Madame Odon and Madame Chasselay. I'm counting on you to liven things up a bit there! Martine Odon's mad about mountaineering, like you, and then there's Madame Chasselay, who ...'

But the arrival of newcomers prevented me from discovering what basic interest I was presumed to have in common with the latter lady, and I never did find out. All I learned later was that she had come to the dinner more or less by chance – she was staying with other guests who felt they couldn't leave her on her own. It didn't matter to me, anyway, and I took my seat at the table without enthusiasm. I was annoyed to be so far from Marion, whose provocative profile I could glimpse occasionally at the other end of the room. Over there, at any rate, Brigitte's art seemed to be working, for Marion's neighbours talked incessantly, causing her to break into merry bursts of laughter whose sound merely increased my sense of isolation and my concealed annoyance.

Personally, I prepared for an evening of boredom – and I'd expected so much of this dinner party too! On my left sat an elderly woman of stern appearance, with a bun of grey hair and a long straight nose, who bore herself stiffly. I couldn't imagine her ever having been 'mad about mountaineering' in any conceivable way, so I concluded, without having to do much detective work, that this must be Madame Chasselay. As for my right-hand neighbour, she had somewhat irregular features, a determined look, and was not much younger than the other lady. I didn't feel in the least inclined to 'liven things up a bit there', nor even to put on much of a show of affability. Luckily dinner began, making any preliminary efforts at conversation unnecessary for the moment. Brigitte had made huge casseroles of duck for her party, and soup-bowls were being passed with much clattering of dishes and shouting of instructions. I was soon absorbed in thoughtfully sipping the broth, savouring its velvety, spicy softness between palate and tongue, and hoping to postpone the moment when casual conversation must be made.

It was my neighbour on the right who broke the silence first. 'I believe you're the mountaineer, Monsieur?' The few remarks we then exchanged were enough to tell me that Madame Odon's contact with genuine mountaineering was distinctly restricted. In point of fact, she went for family rambles in the hills; apart from that, her mountain experience was limited to a few seasons with an outdoor activities organisation, now defunct, which had left her with memories of heroic deeds, all dating back to a surely far-distant past. My replies were polite, but I had not the slightest desire to share still vivid memories of my recent climbing season with her, nor the long list of all my plans for the future.

There was a pause, after which Madame Odon's other neighbour asked her something about communal housing in Russia. He was a professor of geography who, it seemed, was involved with editing an encyclopedia, while she had just spent two years in Moscow; her husband was still working there. This topic of mutual interest caused the two of them to enter upon a series of whispered exchanges, and it looked as if they were well set for the rest of the evening.

Over at the far end of the room, Marion kept on laughing. Brigitte was piling meat and vegetables on fresh plates, which were once again passed from hand to hand.

Then a question from my left-hand neighbour, Madame Chasselay, made me jump.

'Since you're a mountaineer, Monsieur,' she said, 'perhaps you can tell me what happened to my son?'

What a strange question! And what kind of sensible response could I possibly make to such a request, uttered in aggressive tones, on a subject about which I couldn't conceivably have any information? I was momentarily rescued by the arrival of the plates; they needed my attention to keep them moving along and dispatched to the right places. I then busied myself with pouring wine into all the glasses within my reach, vaguely hoping that there would be no follow-up to that peremptory question, which only showed that I didn't know the lady concerned.

She very soon went on: 'My question must have surprised you. I ought to explain. It's about my son – my only son. When he was still quite small, I separated from his father, who died in a road accident not long afterwards. I never remarried; I brought up the child by myself. He needed a great deal of care – he was so highly-strung, so vulnerable and sensitive . . .'

I still couldn't see how my mountaineering experience could have any connection whatsoever with this family history. The name Chasselay meant nothing to me. Of course, my neighbour might have gone back to her maiden name, and there are thousands and thousands of climbers, if her son was really one of them.

'He was such a talented child', his mother went on. 'So hardworking, and so considerate to me! I could go on and on about his thoughtful little ways when he was still small. And he got on so well at school! Everything he did was done thoroughly, and always with success. Oh, we expected so much of him! And then, when he was eighteen, he met the mountains. I say "met" advisedly, Monsieur, because it was just like meeting a person. A person who gave bad advice, a really dreadful influence on him. You sometimes hear talk about this sort of thing; you think it only happens to other people. But that's how it was. In the course of a month's holiday everything changed, everything was turned upside down, and my son abandoned his old habits, his ambitions, his destiny. And me ... even me!'

Madame Chasselay made me feel very uneasy. How on earth could I possibly explain to her? The wonderful feeling of liberation her son must have felt in escaping from a world which was over-organized, too predictable, too constricting. In freeing himself from a mother who treated him as a child who must follow the straight and narrow path she had ordained for him. At a time when he was discovering a totally different world! The walks up to the huts, over crumbling moraines scorched by the midday sun ... the anxiety you suddenly feel when a bank of cirrus clouds appears, possibly heralding bad weather ... happy, chaotic evenings at the hut ... that bitter awakening at dead of night when you must tear oneself from the snug warmth of rough blankets to set out on heaven only knows what kind of adventure. And then the departure, head-torch on, into the shivering darkness . . . the berg-schrunds, fringed with sea-green icicles, the first rays of the sun, revealing the brightly lit landscape in a blaze of glory while the shades of night still linger in the sleeping valleys below ... ice crunching softly under the crampons, the rough rock, the rope uncoiling, the summit attained, the violence of the wind at altitude, the fluffy snow. Your friends, too, and all the jargon of those in the know : AD, V+, cags, gaiters, crabs, friends, prusiks, pegs, flakes, off-widths, gendarmes, schrund, crevasses, fifis, sky hooks, rurps, bongs, copperheads. And the sheer joy of being alive ... how could this methodical mother ever hope to understand any of that? Well, anyway, I knew that I couldn't hand her the key to this universe of ours.

'He started to neglect his studies', she went on. 'He went on working, yes, but so unenthusiastically ... I dreamt of one of the Grandes Écoles for him, but he had to make do with getting into university. He got through all right, got his degree. With such ability, he couldn't fail ... But he wasn't interested any more, he thought of nothing but his mountains! Every weekend, he went off training. And he was filthy when he came back! Ragged, unshaven, his rucksack and his clothes in a disgusting state! It got to the point where our neighbour across the landing pretended not to see him when she passed him on the stairs. I felt so ashamed. He used to be so fastidious about his appearance! And then of course it was off to the mountains every summer. I hardly even got the occasional postcard from somewhere or other. He was camping, naturally. I couldn't have paid for a hotel for him, anyway. How he ever fed himself, all on his own, I don't know ... His friends – well, I never wanted to know them; it would only have encouraged him. Because by now, of course, he had become a very good climber.'

By this time I was feeling a complicated mixture of dislike and pity for my neighbour. Within the boundaries of the narrow world she'd created for herself, she had still felt real pain when she saw her son get away. And it struck me that you never really know much about your own climbing companions, their relatives, even their friends. What surroundings, what atmosphere, what kind of family is back there waiting for them when they get home after the marvels of a climbing season? What reproaches do they come up against, spoken or implied, what anxieties now allayed, perhaps even a show of pride? But whatever, no real comprehension, no understanding!

'I was hoping to see him married, even if that meant losing him in another way,' his mother went on. 'It was about time he went back to taking life a bit more seriously in any case ... I'd arranged for him to meet some girls. Oh no, he had just one idea in his head: he wanted to join some expedition or other going to the Himalayas. The Himalayas, for heaven's sake! But he was afraid they wouldn't take him. So to show how good he was, he went off all by himself, in the middle of winter, to do a big climb on Mont Blanc. The far side of Mont Blanc, if I understood him correctly. A climb nobody had tried before ...'

The dinner went on, but my thoughts were far away. Absent-mindedly, I made little piles of breadcrumbs and then knocked them down with the back of my hand. I was trying to shake off a sort of spell which had come over me, a sense of apprehension that was homing in on me as this tale unfolded, detail following detail while I feared for the fate of the unknown boy about whom I knew nothing, not even his name. But Madame Chasselay went on, quietly:

'Well, of course he succeeded, and he told them so. You see, this was only four years ago. But in spite of what he'd done they didn't pick him, though he was so keen to go. Poor Fabien! There were factions, you see: people like that are no better than anyone else. So he became gloomier than ever, touchier, more withdrawn and bitter. Next summer he left for the mountains, as usual, and guess where he went! To do the same climb as he'd done the winter before. To follow his dream, I suppose. But this time he killed himself.'

I laid my hand on hers. And suddenly it all flashed through my mind
. . . I recognized the story; I knew who she was talking about. Tilbert!
Fabien Tilbert! I'd hardly met him myself, but I'd heard plenty about
him. And if there one thing I would never do it was tell his mother what
really happened to her son.

I remembered a fair-haired lad, thin, rather pale, pleasant enough. His
trouble was that his passion for climbing went hand in hand with quite
exceptional incompetence. It was even said he had no head for heights.
All the same, he put his whole heart into mountaineering, and now I had
a better idea why. Most of his climbs had been failures, but he desperately
wanted to be recognised, to be up there with the best. Then, with
increasing frequency, he began to be suspected of telling tales of imaginary
exploits. Because it was a funny thing, but he always claimed to have
done his major climbs alone or with some chance-met stranger. To put it
bluntly, Fabian Tilbert was making up stories, and he wasn't the first to
do so in the history of mountaineering. And something which might not
have mattered that much became serious when he tried to get selected
for an expedition by claiming a list of routes which he enlarged on as the
fancy took him. It was made clear to him that it wasn't worth pursuing
his application, and he took it badly. Then, following much bullshit and
lavish purchases of equipment, he went missing for a week. A week of
dreadful weather, as it happened, and people were beginning to ask
where he'd got to, when he reappeared, clear-eyed and fresh-faced,
hands intact, claiming for all to hear that he'd made a rather complicated
first ascent in the area of the Innominata. Those familiar with this part of
the world had no trouble in pinning down the errors, contradictions,
and even absurdities in his tale. All he could describe properly was the
walk-in; as for the rest of it, he used fog, snow and storm as reasons for
his inability to give any coherent description of his route. He was even
wrong about the nature of the rock, but he obstinately stuck to his
claims. So they told him, straight out, that no one believed him, and
he'd do better learning to climb properly instead of staging such a
pathetic show. Painful situation, of course, but he'd brought it on
himself. And the fact is that the following summer he wanted to show
the world that he could do this route and prove his detractors in the
wrong. But he just wasn't up to it and he stupidly went and killed
himself.

At least it was a good thing his mother knew only half the story. As for me, what could I do for her except play Tilbert's game myself? I invented things too – what didn't I say! I told her that I'd known her son slightly, that he was a strong climber, that he'd done many famous climbs in terrific style, and with such enjoyment! I said he was remembered in the mountaineering world as a man of great promise, unfortunately cut off in his prime. I said he was a man of the highest ideals. Anything, just anything – but words which, untrue though they were, suddenly brought a smile almost of warmth to Madame Chasselay's stern face. So the image of her son that she would keep was not tarnished. Far from it: I had little doubt that her maternal pride, which must once have burnt so brightly, would find comfort in a memory, softened, embellished.

But life went on. Coffee was served, and another guest, obviously a great expert on the subject, tackled my neighbour on the comparative merits of mocha and arabica. I soon got up and said goodbye to Madame Chasselay, who had retreated into her shell again but silently gave me her hand. Then I left to join the lively group around Marion.

'Been having fun?' asked Brigitte on her way over.

THE ICE FAIRY

A fairy tale for children of today

Once upon a time there was a beautiful fairy, the prettiest creature in the world, so beautiful that you could not set eyes on her without loving her. Her complexion was as white as milk, her mouth was as pink as rhododendrons, and her eyes were so big and blue and pure that you might have thought them two sapphire lakes. In addition, she had a regal but modest look, delicate and attractive features, the bearing of a goddess and the grace of a nymph. She usually wore a dress of silver brocade, its bodice embroidered with precious stones and pearls, and she let her fair, silky hair flow loose over her shoulders in the fashion of those times, wearing on her head only a light wreath of edelweiss with leaves made of diamond. Her palace was built of rock crystal, so that its walls shone like the sun. She used to go out driving in a pretty little painted, gilded sleigh drawn by twenty ptarmigan, harnessed to it with garlands of lace and forget-me-nots. In short, she was the most delightful, charming creature ever seen, and because her godfather, great King Merlin, had given her all the mountain glaciers when she was born, she was known as the Ice Fairy...

Do you believe all that? Well, do you really? If so, then your head's been turned by too much nonsense: too many legends and ridiculous old wives' tales. People don't go in for such fancies nowadays; they show things as they really are. And this is the way things really were:

The Ice Fairy was a rather fat little old woman, who wore her hair in an untidy bun from which several grubby grey locks were always escaping. The complexion of her tanned and weatherbeaten face was blotchy. She wore a large, moth-eaten sweater, a woollen skirt too long for her with a hem that dipped, and very old-fashioned hobnailed boots. She carried an old beige rucksack in which she kept her magic wand.

She went about from glacier to glacier, keeping watch over her flock.

'How's a little glacier today, then?' she would ask. 'Where's my little poppet? Gone beddy-byes, have we? And were we good while Mummy was away? Didn't melt too much? Show Mummy our tongue, then! Good, very good! A glacier's dear little tongue hasn't melted! And have we eaten any nice mountaineers lately? We have? Two? Where did we hide them? Oh, down in the crevasse! Isn't that sweet! There's Mummy's good little glacier, then! Oh, what a pretty, dear, good little glacier it is! Oh, don't its séracs bristle nicely! Mummy's dear little glacier has lovely, lovely séracs. Mummy give it a big kiss! Hang on a moment – what's that? What's that grey stuff on its back? Yuk, how disgusting! How absolutely disgusting! Where did *that* come from? A rock-fall from the Aiguille Plouttaz, was it? The Rock Fairy, up to her tricks again! I'm going to have a word with her if this kind of thing goes on. Old bedbug! Nasty old hag! Bitch! Filthy, foul flibbertigibbet! May demons fly away with her! May Beelzebub have her guts! May radioactivity disintegrate her! How dare she send those horrible rocks falling on Mummy's little glacier, then? Making Mummy's poppet form new moraines – would you believe it? There, there, calm down, my little pet. You stop there and be a good glacier. I'm off to consult the Snow Fairy.'

The Snow Fairy was a cantankerous, ugly old thing; beside her, the Ice Fairy seemed relatively attractive. She invariably wore old-fashioned, mottled plus-fours, their seat worn out from much sliding downhill on her bottom and showing knickers stained green. An American army surplus anorak covered her thin torso, and she protected her bald pate with a washed-out cap embellished with a big brown plastic eye-shade, in an attempt to give her watery, rheumy eyes some kind of protection. A prickly moustache decked her upper lip, adding an ill-judged finishing touch to a face which was frankly nothing to write home about. The Snow Fairy had adapted her wand to make it into a kind of pick – half walking stick, half ski stick – and she used it for getting around her domain as well as casting spells. She was a great friend of the Ice Fairy, and they transacted a lot of business in ice and snow together.

'Hi there, old girl!' said the Ice Fairy, hailing her. 'How are isotherms doing? Holding up all right? Paying good dividends in snow? Splendid, glad to hear it, but that's enough shop talk. Let me tell you what brings me here. Would you believe it, that bitch of a Rock Fairy has sent another big rock-fall down on one of my glaciers! She's the pits! Always at it! The moment I turn my back, down they come. It really is too bad; I'm fed up to here with the old harpy! She needs the Evil Eye cast on her to keep her from doing harm! You're always so full of bright ideas – help me!'

The Snow Fairy smiled, showing the stumps of her decayed old teeth.

'Okay,' she grunted. 'But one good turn deserves another. You come and help me balance the snowflake accounts next winter, and I'll think up some way to put that old cow out of action. Is it a deal? Done!

Now, let's see, let's see ... hm ... well, well, well, I do believe I've had a real little gem of an idea! It involves Crowcuss. Here's what we could do ... '

Hissing, hawking and spluttering, the Snow Fairy whispered her diabolical plan into her accomplice's ear.

A cavernous laugh greeted her words. The Ice Fairy liked the alluring plan.

'We must start by going to see her,' she said immediately. 'Ready?'

The two cronies sat on the slope, one behind the other, each holding her magic wand. Sliding, tumbling, somersaulting and bouncing over crevasses and bergschrunds, they were soon at the bottom of a vast glacial amphitheatre.

'Oh, I can take this opportunity to see that little baby again!' exclaimed the Ice Fairy, her maternal instincts in full flow once more. 'Oh, isn't it a pretty baby! Mummy's little sweetie, then! Has it widdled in the mountain stream like a good glacier? Oh, what a love it is! There's Mummy's dear little glacie-wacie, then! And the nice Snow Fairy-Wairy will give it a lovely big ballie-wallie of powder snow to play with!'

'Sez you!' interrupted that lady. 'As if I'd nothing better to do than make ballie-wallies for Mummy's little glacie-wacies! Such nonsense! You spoil those glaciers of yours rotten! If I was half as soppy as you with my snowfields, my life wouldn't be worth living. They wouldn't hold for a moment. They'd send avalanches pissing down all over the place! Glaciers, my dear girl, are like snowfields: you have to keep a good watch on them or they'll go right out of control. They start by doing exactly as they please, and then – '

But the Ice Fairy was not listening to this wise advice.

'Bye-bye, then, my little poppet,' she said. 'See you soon! Give Mummy a big, big kiss with your tonguie-wunguie! Ooh, isn't it a little scamp! It tickled its Mummy!'

'Is its Mummy ever going to get a move on?' inquired the Snow Fairy impatiently. 'Or is she waiting for more rocks to fall on her little poppets?'

'All right, all right, I'm coming! Such impatience! You just don't understand. Domes and gullies and snow caps and so forth simply don't have the character of a dear, sweet, chubby little glacier. If I were to tell you ... oh, very well, very well! All right, keep your hair on! Let's go!'

The two fairies continued on their way to the foot of a tall needle of granite, inside which the Rock Fairy had fixed herself up a cave. The place was as good as inaccessible. The only way in was by hauling yourself up a dangling rope, which the Rock Fairy wound in by means of an ingenious mechanical device when she didn't need to use it.

'Yoohoo!' shouted the two old fairies, hypocritically. 'Yoohoo! Surprise! We've come calling!'

The Rock Fairy leaned out of her cave, looking suspicious.

'I say, we should have brought her a present!' said the Snow Fairy.

'I've got a broken ice-axe in my bag,' whispered the Ice Fairy. 'Found it in a crevasse. I might as well give it to her. I've got eight hundred and seventy-nine more just like it at home.'

'We've brought you a present!' shouted the Snow Fairy.

'Oh yeth?' enquired the Rock Fairy, who had lisped ever since a block of stone knocked her front teeth out.

'An ice-axe! A lovely new ice-axe – a famous make. Hardly broken at all!'

The Rock Fairy found fewer ice-axes in her territory than the Snow Fairy or the Ice Fairy did. Plenty of pegs, crabs and nuts, yes, but not all that many ice-axes. Furthermore, she was grasping, and loved getting little presents for free.

'Let'th have a look!' she said, cautiously.

'Nasty old cow!' grumbled the Ice Fairy, opening her bag. 'And talk about mean! Doesn't even trust her fellow fairies. I ask you!'

'All right. I'll thend the rope down!' called the Rock Fairy a moment later.

Hauling themselves up over the smooth stone by main force, the other two muttered disagreeable remarks to each other.

'You'd have to be really cracked to live up there!'

'It's a tip, too! Dark and dirty and full of pebbles. Right behind the times.'

'She's a real old bat! I never could abide the old hag!'

But once they arrived, society manners took over.

'What a nice place you have here!' exclaimed the visitors in unison. 'Oh, how prettily you've done it up! And what a wonderful position! That view!'

'Let'th thee your ithe-ackth!' demanded the Rock Fairy.

'Of course, of course! Here we are. There, it's for you, dear! I felt sure you hadn't got one as good as that yet!'

'I've got thome jutht ath broken!' said the Rock Fairy, sarcastically.

'Oh, now wait a minute! You haven't looked at the pick and the adze! It's practically new. Not damaged by its fall, except the shaft, just a little, but that's all. You're never going to get stroppy over a few chips, are you?'

'Oh, all right! I'll have it!' grumbled the Rock Fairy. 'Well, what newth? I thuppothe you haven't heard the weather forecatht?'

'No change,' replied the Snow Fairy, diplomatically; she was well aware that a drop in temperature and several snow showers were expected. 'Going to carry on pretty much as it is. What are you making in your cauldron?'

'Quartz thoup!' said the Rock Fairy. 'I won't offer you any. It'th not done yet. My own thpecial rethipe: thpithed with clay, a little amethytht for colour, and fried shale added at the latht minute!'

'Brilliant!' cried the other two. 'Sounds delicious.'

'It'th not bad!' said the Rock Fairy, modestly.

But we haven't yet described the lady in question. The Rock Fairy was no beautiful bronzed climber, slender of figure, with supple muscles rippling under the stretch fibre of a one-piece climbing suit. Far from it. She was a tall, thin, gangling creature, bent almost double with age. Her spindly legs were clad in patched old cords. A grey jacket, a battered cap, and climbing boots riddled with holes lent her a distinctly eccentric appearance. Her nutcracker chin almost met her hooked nose, a meeting facilitated by the fact that her jaw, injured by numerous falling rocks, now contained almost none of the thirty-two teeth originally bestowed on it by Nature and consequently took up very little room. Under sooty brows, her sharp eyes shone like agate, which was not surprising, since they *were* agate.

Near his mistress, claws clinging to a pointed rock, sat Crowcuss, an Alpine chough as old as Methuselah, but still in robust health. He was feared all over the mountain.

'Handsome as ever, I see, Crowcuss!' remarked the Snow Fairy.

'Caw!' replied the bird amiably, letting some droppings fall on the visitor's cap.

'Ithn't he funny?' exclaimed the Rock Fairy. 'You never know what he'll get up too. Gueth what? Up on the Aiguille Fache the other day he cut the cord holding a mountaineer'th rope with hith little beak all by himthelf, jutht for fun!'

'Oh, that was Crowcuss, was it?' inquired the Ice Fairy without much interest. 'I found the mountaineer in my bergschrund. In pieces; not very tidy. You're a litter lout, Crowcuss!'

'Well now,' said the Rock Fairy, cheered by the memory of this incident, 'what can I give you to drink? Gypthum fizz? Granite protogine? Feldthpar on the rockth? With thome little pudding-thtoneth to nibble!'

Soon the three fairies were feasting greedily, exchanging polite remarks and venomous glances. Then, as night came on, they said goodbye to each other, and the visitors slid down the rope to the foot of the rock.

'What an impossible place to get in and out of!' grumbled the Snow Fairy. 'I've torn my trousers.'

'And my stomach's churning,' groaned the Ice Fairy. 'Must be her horrible pudding-stones.'

'It certainly was her pudding-stones,' agreed her friend. 'Old as the hills and crumbling! I didn't notice till too late, when I realized she was hardly eating a thing. Finishing up her left-overs on us, the mean old hag!'

'Yuk!' said the Ice Fairy. 'I'm not surprised. She was acting too nice to be true. But what about the rest of it? Do you think it'll work?'

'Yes, I think so. I cast the spell on her mechanism while she fixed the drinks. It ought to come into effect in a few hours' time, like we planned. And it's a modern curse, one she won't know. You have to use a binary code to break it. That sort of thing's not her line. You'll have everything ready to do your bit?'

'I will! I don't like sacrificing nice new séracs, chucking them away down the mountainside, but it can't be helped! Right, I'll see to that while you lie low here, as agreed, and then we meet as soon as possible in the Mont Chervole bergschrund.'

'Okay, here we go, then!' said the Snow Fairy. 'And make it good and noisy!'

It was indeed a tremendous rumbling roar that woke the Rock Fairy in the middle of the night.

'What on earth ith that?' she exclaimed.

'Caw! Caw! Caw!' shrieked Crowcuss, who hated having his sleep disturbed. 'Caw! Caw! Caw!'

'Shut up, Crowcuth dear!' said the Rock Fairy. 'I'll have to go and thee what'th up, and pretty quick too, but I won't take you. You need your beauty thleep. Conthidering all the racket, that rock-fall can't be very far away, tho I won't be long. Go back to thleep, pet.'

Quick as a flash, she slipped down the rock-face and then spoke the magic charm which wound the rope in and out. But the rope did not budge.

'Oh, bother! It'th thtuck!' cursed the old fairy. 'And I've no time to fikth it. Never mind. Thith won't take long, and there'th nobody roaming around here at night.'

Striding out, she hurried off to inspect the damage. Judging by the direction from which the noise came, the rock-fall seemed to have been on the slopes of the Aiguille Clottaz. If so, thought the Rock Fairy, that stupid clot the Ice Fairy had got her séracs off balance. Silly old fool! Why didn't she mind her own business, instead of paying social calls on other people and finishing up their feldspar? Because that was what she'd done, the old soak, finished every last bit of it!

Meanwhile, however, a shadowy figure was lurking at the bottom of the rope. A brown figure with a big eye-shade, and plus-fours drawn in at mid-calf. The intruder briskly seized the rope and hauled herself swiftly up to the cave.

'Caw!' squawked Crowcuss.

But he could say no more. A powerful sleeping draught was tipped into his beak while a thick hood came down over his head. Next moment he had been stuffed into a bag and was on his way down the rope with his kidnapper.

They were only just in time. The Rock Fairy arrived very soon afterwards in a filthy temper, having just found out that an avalanche of séracs had covered a whole schist slope of which she thought highly. She seized the rope in her own turn, climbed up to her cave, and then tried to wind the rope in.

'Bother! It really ith thtuck!' she grumbled. 'And I can't thay the magic thpell; if I talk too loud it'll wake Crowcuth. Better go to bed now. I'll put thingth right in the morning.'

On getting up she did indeed go straight to the rope, and as the spell was now broken she wound it in quite easily. Then she turned back to the cave, and the smile on her toothless mouth turned to a grimace of horror.

'Crowcuth!' she shouted. 'Where'th Crowcuth gone?'

Crowcuss's wings were too rheumaticky for him to undertake long flights by himself. He never went any great distance except on his mistress's shoulder. After searching frantically she had to face the facts: Crowcuss had disappeared!

Meanwhile, in the Mont Chervole bergschrund, the Ice Fairy and the

Snow Fairy were doubled up with mirth at the thought of the trick they had played on their colleague. Lying beside them, tied up with a bit of old doubled cord, Crowcuss was perfectly reconciled to his adventure, thanks to the billycans of provisions placed near him by the two old fairies – provisions which had slipped from the hands or rucksacks of mountaineers. Stuffing himself non-stop, he didn't even dream of letting out one of his formidable caws.

The Rock Fairy turned her cave upside down, and eventually found a piece of tent canvas lying in a corner. It had a message written on it.

'Old Whitch!' said this missive. 'Wee hav kidnaped yore horribul burd Crowcuss. Wee ar finking ov eting him, ore purhapps wee wil giv him bak too yoo. Butt iff we doo yoo mussed leev thee roks allone. Yors sinsearly. The Browniez ov thee morain.'

'What the dickenth?' yelped the Rock Fairy. 'Who *are* the brownieth of the moraine? I never heard of any thuch people! You don't know where you are nowadayth! They mutht have climbed up that wretched rope, after I didn't bother to wind it in. What a meth! Thuch a thing would never have happened in the old dayth. You're not thafe in your own cave at night now! Oh, the little horrorth! And to think it'th me who feedth the moraineth! Eat Crowcuth! Huh! They'll find him tough, in any cathe. What'th to be done? Oh, what *ith* to be done?'

She thought about it for a long, long time. On further reflection, she vaguely thought she remembered hearing her grandmother mention the brownies of the moraine. But why on earth would they want her to leave the rocks alone? Why should they mind if rocks fell or didn't fall? Rock-falls made more moraines, so it was pure profit as far as they were concerned ... unless they had the job of taking a census of the pebbles, in which case it was true that she was giving them a lot of extra work. But what fun it was, sending large and slightly crumbling sections of mountainside tumbling down, revealing new slopes full of surprises beneath them! What fun it was to scatter debris all over the glaciers and snowfields ruled by those two old hags! Nobbling the clouds, the air, the winds, the mists and the sky itself, persuading them to go easy with the snow that fed the other fairies' domains! But then there was Crowcuss! Crowcuss! She couldn't live without him: his mutinous squawks, his macabre little practical jokes, his affectionate pecks.

All of a sudden a kind of greyish missile shot through the mouth of the cave and landed at her feet. It was half a crampon, with another message tied to its points.

'Hi yoo old batt!' she read. 'Wee hop yoo hav thort itt ovr. Meenwile heer iz a fevver fromm yore horribul burd and wee wil pul owt orl thee otherz iff yoo dont promiss too leeve thee rox alone. Iff yoo agree then leeve a bigg tchunk ov kwartz on the glaysier tabul beloe. Yores sinsearly. Thee Browniez ov the morain.'

This was getting serious! One of Crowcuss's feathers! The poor darling! Even worse, in view of its condition it seemed to be a tail feather he had lost, and that must have hurt him quite a bit. She must get Crowcuss back before he was down to bare skin and bone. But the Rock Fairy had a serious problem, which no one suspected. Not only was old age beginning to make her forgetful, she had also mislaid her book of magic spells, and of course she couldn't remember where she might have put it. All that she could call to mind were a few charms and elementary curses, things her grandmother had taught her when she was little and which did no more than allow her to keep up appearances. Casting a spell on the brownies was beyond her; so was calling up the image of Crowcuss in a magic mirror. She'd have had to ask those two old pests the Ice Fairy and the Snow Fairy for help, and she couldn't admit such weaknesses to them, let alone the fact that any such plan was logically doomed to failure: the stale pudding-stones she had given them must have had a shocking effect on their digestions and they'd have worked out why, which would make their cooperation very unlikely, not to say dangerous. Besides, wouldn't a long rest allow her to recover some strength? And enough memory to recall a few more spells? Who knew, she might even remember in what hole or crevice she'd hidden that wretched magic book! The more she thought about it, the better the idea seemed. Of course, her rocks would lose ground if she wasn't constantly at work. But that would only make it more fun, a few thousand years hence, to recover the ground they'd lost. She opened her larder and rummaged about in it for a large lump of quartz which she could leave on the glacier table at dusk.

'Wretched little brownieth!' she thought. 'But they've done me a thervithe without meaning to!'

She acted at once. At dawn, a demanding 'Caw! rent the air, and the Rock Fairy rushed out to find Crowcuss in the moraine adjoining the foot of her granite needle, in better voice than ever.

'We're going to have a little retht, Crowcuth!' announced his mistress. 'We're going to bed, and we'll thtay there for quite a time. We'll thtart work again in due courthe, but now it'th time for bed. I promithe you we won't thuffer for it! There'll be thome terrific rock-fallth later!'

Meanwhile the Ice Fairy could no longer rest idle. She went to put the big quartz crystal on the highest of her hanging glaciers, like a trophy.

'Oh, poor little poppet, it's gone all thinny-winny!' she exclaimed. 'If it's a very, very good little glacier, Mummy will give it a lovely surprise. Lots of nice snowie-wowie! Lots of lovely icie-wicie! It'll get to be a big, big glacier and flow all the way down to the valley. There now, who's going to give his Mummy a great big kissie-wissie?'

And so it was that the Great Ice Age of the third millennium AD began.

CANDORE-SUR-NANT

She leaned over the balcony and contemplated the sleeping village. A few moments earlier, around eleven o'clock, groups of people coming out of the small cinema had briefly enlivened the square before sauntering off into the night. Now Catherine could see nothing except doorways and closed shutters, faintly illuminated by the light from a street-lamp filtering through the leaves of a tree. The peaceful scene resembled a theatre set except that, above the roofs and above the black outline of the mountains which bordered the valley, a few distant stars were twinkling in a vast velvety sky.

In the room behind her the children were breathing gently, deep in the profound sleep of the young, but she herself did not feel at all sleepy. Driving always left her in a tense state which she found hard to shake off. And then she wanted to savour this return to Candore-sur-Nant to the full. It had come so unexpectedly, twenty-four years after her first and only visit to the place. But there must be secret corners of the mind where memories are preserved, for to her surprise she recognised innumerable details from the past which had certainly never come into her head since then.

She had left Paris the day before, with her three children, to travel to Barcelonnette by a roundabout route. It was the start of the holidays. The cornfields swayed under a gentle breeze, and the grassy banks were studded with poppies and the starry clusters of cow parsley. Little clouds like turtle-doves floated in the clear blue sky. Summer insects crashed into the windscreen. They chose out-of-the-way roads, visited ancient churches and castles and picnicked in clearings in the woods, having followed a maze of tracks and lanes, some barely suitable for motor vehicles. High-spirited childish squabbling filled the car. And what a series of obstacles had to be overcome before they finished up at Candore-sur-Nant that evening! As they approached the Alps, lorry-drivers were blocking the road; there was a lengthy diversion. Sulks from Mathilde who, in the superior wisdom of her fifteen years, could not accept their leaving the road she had wanted to take. Weariness setting in and making Jérôme, in the back, start annoying Julie. Catherine gave the map to her son to keep him occupied and simultaneously avoid offending her eldest child, since Mathilde as navigator would have looked for various villages with tourist shops, as usual. Jérôme, on the other hand, proud of his new job, launched into a hectic recital of countless names of villages along their route.

'Arqueyre! Châline! Chaumeron-les-Bornes! Varlange! Creusy! Touvenod! La Torrière! Bardeille! Candore-sur-Nant!'

'Candore-sur-Nant ... is it far?' Catherine had asked.

'Hang on. Eight here ... then fifteen ... It must add up to around forty kilometres. No, maybe I'm wrong ... Anyway, we shouldn't have much further to go tomorrow to get over the pass called ... called ...'

'But I want to go to Châline!' Julie had wailed. 'I want to go to Châline!'

'Be quiet, Julie!' Catherine had told her. 'Jérôme, tell me where to turn off for Candore-sur-Nant, please.'

And so it was decided, and the memories immediately started to crowd in. She thought they could always book in at that little hotel...

However, the place had changed. There were a great many hotels now, but they all seemed to be full up at this late hour of the evening. Catherine was glad to take the first room on offer where they could put up a camp-bed for Julie and add an air-mattress for Jérôme.

Candore-sur-Nant! More than half her life had passed since the one time she had been here before. She was a student then, and after a stupid incident involving a bivouac and frost-bite, her parents were reluctant to let her return to the mountains and made it a specific condition that she must take a guide. These days she had a better notion of all the sacrifices she had asked them to make, the anxiety they must have felt in spite of everything.

Martial Tramelan was the guide who accompanied her most often. Although he had a long list of climbs to his credit, he had not lost his sense of adventure and liked looking for fresh summits and routes which were new to him. Catherine was delighted to take part in this quest of the unknown. At Candore-sur-Nant there was only one climb worthy of the name, the North Face of Mont Vague. The usual route up the mountain was no more than a long, mild snow-plod, and the white billows of the neighbouring mountains appeared more suitable for ski-tours than summer climbs. But in the middle of this gentle range there reared up, like a gash, the north face of the mountain, all broken rock and ice, nearly a thousand metres high. You climbed it on the right, where you could see the outlines of a steep gully which ended below the summit, on the west ridge. No one had yet attempted the direct route, with its sérac barrier and its mass of craggy vertical rocks, unstable as a pile of dinner plates.

As she recalled these memories, the years melted away. Standing at her open window, Catherine was no longer the mother of a family, going on holiday with her nearly grown-up children. Far from it she suddenly felt twenty-four years younger. It was only yesterday she had been trudging towards the gaping bergschrund in the moonlight ... only yesterday she was moving slowly up the dark, freezing slope. The conditions had not been good. The ice was not far away, under a thin layer of unstable snow. They often had to belay if they were to make any progress ... then they had emerged on the ridge, in the sunshine, and had followed it to the summit. It was Catherine's second climb of the season, as she remembered, and one of her boots was hurting her ankle. The descent by the normal route had seemed to go on for ever, and so did the path which led down to Candore-sur-Nant ... she had stopped for a moment, to cool her face in the stream. Once again, she seemed to feel the icy water on her hands, her forehead, her cheeks, the drops running down her neck. Finally, when they reached the village and before they set off again, she and Martial had sat down on the terrace of the only hotel, to drink an orangeade, two orangeades, three orangeades! The landlord had joked about their thirst. He asked them where they had been, and congratulated the girl on her achievement. And so that discussion between him and Martial began. Martial loved to make people talk, ask them questions, learn from them. He had his own special way of winning the confidence of the people he talked to other guides, hut wardens, farm workers, café owners or garage mechanics – and he knew how to glean interesting information from them about mountains, places, people and parish affairs.

Last winter, of course, Catherine had remembered that conversation, but she had too much else on her mind at the time to linger over memories or indulge in lengthy musings. It must have been around Christmas, when they were moving house and Julie had mumps. For at least two weeks Catherine was snowed under with work and worries. She kept up with the latest news through the radio and newspaper headlines, but she registered it only in a detached sort of way, and while she felt genuine sympathy for the victims, she was soon absorbed by her own preoccupations again.

Whereas this evening, when a series of coincidences and a sudden urge had brought her back to Candore-sur-Nant, she was able to let her thoughts roam free. A question from the past may sometimes receive a belated answer in this way, or over the course of time various events may link together to make a whole, more strangely than might at first appear. Tomorrow, before they left, she would look for the old hotel.

On that previous visit she had kept out of the conversation between Martial and the hotel-keeper. It was men's talk anyway. But she had listened with interest, feeling a sense of well-being caused by the break, the rest, and the refreshing shade.

'This is the first time I've been here,' Martial had said. 'Nice little resort. The setting's beautiful, with walks and some high-mountain scenery. But you don't get many visitors. Why not try developing the place? You need two or three ski-lifts – that'd bring people here in winter.'

'My own idea precisely!' exclaimed the landlord. 'I keep telling the locals so. And there's our weather too; a sort of micro-climate, you might say. It's fine here when the weather's filthy eight or ten kilometres away! This could be a really attractive resort. In fact I'm expecting it to be just that!'

'This hotel is yours?'

'It certainly is, and that's saying something ... You don't mind?'

Now in full flow, the hotelier had taken a chair and sat down at their table.

'I started when I was quite young. I was the eldest of six, you see, and my parents found me a place as kitchen boy in a restaurant as soon as they could. That way they had one less mouth to feed. I used to peel potatoes, scrub floors, do odd jobs, anything ... and suddenly I began to like it. I felt this was my scene, and I think I decided right from the start to do my best to get to the top. I put what I earned into a savings account. That meant more to me than going to the movies or hanging about with my mates. I had my plan. I steadily improved my knowledge of the business. I was well liked, because people could see I was willing. I worked in several hotels. That's how I met my wife; she was working as a chambermaid. The two of us soon came to an understanding, being so similar. We both wanted to succeed; we saved all our money, and did what was necessary to make more, never clock-watching, always keen to see how things worked, buying manuals to teach us book-keeping. Right from the start we'd decided: only one child! And then, when we'd got where we wanted ... Dadou! Where are you, Dadou?'

A merry little face had appeared from below the terrace. Two bright eyes. A shock of tousled brown hair. Grazed knees, painted with Mercurochrome ...

'Wipe your nose, Dadou!'

Dadou wiped his nose. Then, as Catherine was giving him a little smile, he stole a glance at his father to check that he wasn't looking and wickedly stuck out a huge pink tongue, before disappearing under the terrace again to carry on with those mysterious activities which absorb little boys.

'And we succeeded! We stuck to our plan!' his father went on. 'Like I said, we had it all worked out even before we married ... I wanted my own hotel, and one child to inherit it no problems over the inheritance then, or over dividing up the property once I'm gone. That's me, you see: well organized!'

'I can see you are,' Martial had agreed.

'And we did manage to buy the hotel, eight years ago. The bank lent us the money to complete the purchase, and we're paying it back. It was a real bargain, this hotel, being in rather a backwater at the time, but I saw straight away you could make something of it, and of the village too. It's our whole life! I work in the kitchen, my wife looks after the reception and all the rest. During the season we hire a local girl to serve at table and help with the bedrooms. Everything's polished, gleaming, clean and welcoming. But the resort does need to expand!'

'People come in winter?'

'They do, they certainly do! But not as many as there ought to be. And they tend to be retired people, or small families. It isn't as if they were piste skiers with big appetites, wanting food and drink and plenty of après-ski activities. I often discuss it with the locals. Of course they still see me as a bit of an outsider, but I think they appreciate me. We get on all right, but they're peasants, all the same. They'd gain a lot from some new facilities here, but they won't listen. Of course I know this place will never be a really, really big resort, but I'd be quite happy with the sort of thing you were suggesting. We need to instal some ski-lifts and develop the tourist industry properly. Maybe have a few guides who could give ski lessons in winter. And get ourselves known, that's the main thing, through some publicity or even better, a nice accident!'

'A nice accident?' said Martial, surprised.

'Well, don't get me wrong, will you, but I know what I'm talking about. I've studied the way these things happen. Look, the North Face of Mont Vague, that's dangerous. But you two came down all right. Good thing for you, of course, but not so good for us. That north face is climbed twice a year at the most and nothing ever happens. Well, now, suppose a party of three, say, fell from near the top? No, no – don't frown like that, Mademoiselle! I'm not ill-wishing anyone, least of all you. In fact I wish the climbers the best of luck. It could be an English party, though, or Germans someone who doesn't matter!'

'Weird ideas you have!' said Martial, and heaved a sigh.

'Not simply ideas – I see what goes on. It needs only one accident to get a place into the news! The name of Mont Vague would be in all the papers in big black type. And so would the name of Candore-sur-Nant! Everywhere! Candore-sur-Nant! Candore-sur-Nant! The tourist office, assuming there was one, would have to spend millions to get the same result! Candore-sur-Nant! Candore-sur-Nant! Candore-sur-Nant! From our special correspondent in Candore-sur-Nant . . . I can see it now! We'd become a household name world-wide, without spending a penny on advertising. We'd be on radio too! And television!'

An odd character, that hotelier. He insisted on standing them the last round of drinks, and asked Martial to mention Mont Vague to his friends.

Well, all that was long ago; it was ancient history now. Twenty-four years had passed, and here she was, back at a window in Candore-sur-Nant, her children asleep behind her. She realized that the place had indeed grown much bigger, through the gradual development which has affected so many small villages in the Alps, and without the help of that famous accident! The accident had happened all the same, but later, showing that Martial was right, and a good situation was enough in itself. Yes, she'd send Martial a postcard tomorrow, with a view of the resort as it looked today. Or no, a view of the North Face of Mont Vague. She would show it to the children and describe the route to them. She wouldn't mention the accident. They must have heard about it last winter, but they'd have forgotten the name of the mountain. Wincing suddenly, Catherine wondered if it had given the area publicity. Well, yes, it must have done. How awful awful, but that's life. And the resort must be so full because it all happened during the last Christmas holiday. Back here on the spot, she could visualize the drama better, so close to the ski-runs, the restaurants, the bars. She couldn't remember the details very well, but she was aware of the outlines of the story, and you always feel concerned if you've been involved with the mountains yourself, part of that world. Two daring climbers had attempted the first direct ascent, in winter, when the loose rock would be held in place by the ice. That made sense. But they had run into a problem and got stuck, and then the storm broke over them. There was no way of reaching them on that massive, steep mountain wall beset by fog and snow, inaccessible even by helicopter. One of the rescuers had died as well ... The whole business caused controversy: bitter and moreover pointless arguments. Catherine pictured the deaths of those men, alone and in pain, so close to the ski lessons, the warm houses, the lavishly laden tables. No one should ever wish for an accident She shivered. The church clock struck. Half-past twelve! High time for bed!

Next morning they had a good breakfast and prepared to go for a walk round the village. Catherine wrote her postcard to Martial, got a stamp and then, followed by the children, headed for the centre to look for the old hotel. It had hardly changed, but it now had an impressive addition in the shape of the modern wing on the right. There it was, just as she remembered it, spick and span, with pink pebble-dash and grey shutters, and the same old-fashioned terrace with its wrought-iron railings. Catherine went in. A large, jovial man was sitting in Reception.

'Are you the owner?' she asked.

'I am indeed. You want somewhere to stay with your brood here?'

'No, that's not it ... We're leaving, just passing through. Forgive me, but the fact is I stopped here once, a long time ago. You don't happen to know what happened to the man who used to own the hotel?'

'Knew him, did you? I'm afraid you're too late, madam. He sold the place to me only this spring. He'd had enough of it, didn't want to stay any longer. He was mayor here, you know, but he resigned. That accident, it was such a blow. Just think of it! ... His only son ... '

A TRUE STORY

This is another mountaineering story, it's a fantastic story, and it's a true story.

It so happens that I've thought up and written quite a number of Alpine stories with an element of fantasy, and as a result I've been asked I don't know how many times whether I've ever had any out-of-the-ordinary experiences myself. People seemed to think I had only to set foot on a glacier to attract any number of ghosts, demons and fairies, with instant manifestations of supernatural phenomena in the very real world of high altitude. Of course I always replied in the negative, dismissing from my mind a certain incident on the Matterhorn which I did not think worth mentioning.

Once, however, that question was put to me in a stranger and more urgent manner.

It was on 11 February 1983, in Grenoble. I was there to receive the Prix de l'Alpe award for my first collection of stories, *Flammes de Pierre*. The woman who was in touch with me had organized a discussion to mark the occasion. It was to take place at the big F.N.A.C. book hypermarket; I think she worked there. This was at the period when the F.N.A.C. still took an interest in bookselling, a field it neglects now that it has turned to more commercial projects. But that's another story ...

To get back to this woman; I had never met her before, and have never seen her since. She was of German origin, and was called Erika. I forget her surname.

Before the afternoon discussion, Erika had invited me to lunch in a restaurant on an embankment of the Isère, below the slopes of the Fort de la Bastille. We began talking. And then she asked her question.

As usual I laughed and said, no, most certainly not! I'd come across moraines full of pebbles in the mountains, and powder snow, steep faces and ridges, blue ice and forbidding rocks, but I assured her all this was well within the most ordinary norms of real experience, although cold weather and gusts of sleet-laden wind might sometimes turn a climb into a small hell, while on other occasions the light streaming in golden rays from the clouds, the turquoise sky and the firm snow made me more inclined to think of paradise.

For Erika's benefit, however, I did briefly mention what had happened on the Matterhorn:

'The mountain was covered with fresh snow, and the weather was very uncertain. We oughtn't to have gone ... But sometimes you set out just to have a look. And as we climbed on, conditions got worse. Below the Solvay Hut, where most accidents happen, the rock slabs were invisible. My companion decided to climb on a little further alone. We were still roped, but the rope was no use, since there was nothing to fasten it to. The structure of the Matterhorn resembles a set of overlapping scales facing the wrong way, or the shingles of a roof ... When my climbing companion reached a spot eight or ten metres above me, the powder slipped, or a hold gave way, or well, I don't know exactly what happened, but he began to fall. I was utterly powerless, and it was only on principle that I kept the rope clamped around my shoulder. As he tried to check himself and get some kind of hold he tore his nails, but he couldn't stop, and went on falling. He passed me at high speed and continued falling down the slope. By now he had turned to face the void. There was a drop of about a thousand metres below us. I remained very lucid, although I knew there was no hope left. I was waiting for the moment when the rope would inevitably snatch me away. But at the precise instant when it ran out, and I was surely going to be carried off too, no such thing happened. I didn't feel even the slightest jolt. The fall was halted when it had become unstoppable, as if some mysterious hand had pulled everything up short. There was no explanation! I've been lucky quite a few times in my life, but that day I felt I'd experienced a miracle.'

'I hope you turned back then?'

'Of course not! I hate failures. We went on! We climbed in what was practically a storm, come what may ... And we didn't come back down, safe and sound, until we'd completed our climb.'

There was silence. When you mention an incident like that, it produces a sort of hesitation or awkwardness. That's why one seldom speaks of such things.

'Well, I have a story to tell you too,' said Erika. 'A story which is perfectly true and certainly supernatural. It happened to my grandfather, and I heard it from his own lips.'

'You mean a true fantasy? In the mountains?'

'Yes! I felt sure you'd be interested.'

'Indeed I would! And your grandfather was the protagonist?'

'Well, at least he was very closely involved in the whole business ... It happened in a Bavarian village around the early part of this century.

In the twenties, probably. There was a whole group of young peasants who were keen mountaineers, seven or maybe eight of them. They worked hard on the farms and in the fields during the week, and every Sunday they used to meet and go climbing together on rock walls, or skiing in winter... I don't say they were brilliant climbers, or opened up exceptional routes, but they loved their long expeditions, and the entire band was united by deep friendship. Sometimes they'd go miles to another valley for a change, spending the night in one of the rustic huts you found in those times and setting out to climb a new peak next day. They would get home the following night, weary but intoxicated with happiness, high altitude, and their mutual affection, in a very happy frame of mind. This went on for several years, and as time passed the friendship between them became closer and closer.'

'I can imagine it. One of the benefits of youth...'

'Well, one day one of them got engaged and stopped climbing with the group. He'd fallen for a girl in a neighbouring village. His name was Ulrich and hers was Constanze. The two of them were madly in love, which didn't suit his friends... "Come on, Ulrich," they used to say, "you've got plenty of time before you tie yourself down like that... We're young! Life is good... Surely you aren't going to drop us for a girl!" But Ulrich loved Constanze and Constanze loved Ulrich. They were married in the little baroque church whose onion dome towered over the village. The young couple were radiant with happiness when they came out, dressed in the velvet costumes still worn at that period. And everyone applauded the handsome pair, even the friends Ulrich had forsaken. "Well!" said one of them simply, during the festivities that followed, "getting married needn't stop you coming back to climb with us!" "I promised Stanzi never to leave her, and I'll keep my word!" he replied.'

'And did he?'

'Oh yes! Much to the annoyance of his companions, because he was the most daring of them all, the strongest and the most cheerful. Only now he was perfectly happy living with his beloved Constanze and wouldn't leave her. A summer and a winter passed like this. Spring came back, spangling the fields with flowers and melting the high snows. The couple were expecting a child, and they loved each other more than ever... One day, however, when the young men of the village were preparing for a good long expedition in a distant valley, they came to see Ulrich. "Come on!" they said. "It's over a year since you went climbing with us. A man can't spend his whole life tied to a woman's apron strings, however charming she is. We really do like your Constanze, but her baby isn't due for another two months. She won't be in any danger if you're away. And she'll be in the care of her your parents too. So come with us for a route on Saturday and Sunday, why don't you? It'll be the last before you're a father, and we're as pleased about that as you are. Aren't we right, Stanzi? Let us have him once more, one last time ... " The young woman saw that her husband was tempted, and she smiled lovingly. "Go on, Ulrich!" she said. "They're right. You'd like to see the mountains again, and after that we'll never be parted again, just as we promised each other. " '

'And he let them persuade him?'

'Yes, although he felt a little remorseful, but it's true he was tempted by the prospect of a couple of days' good climbing. He got up early on the Saturday morning, saw to a few jobs about the farm, had a solid breakfast of bread, soup and cheese, strapped his sack to his back, described his route to Constanze in detail once more, and told her when he expected to be back, late in the evening of the next day. Then he kissed her and left.'

'Oh dear! I have a nasty presentiment about your story! I'm sure Ulrich had an accident!'

'Not a bit of it! In fact the expedition went rather well. All the young men were together again, including my grandfather. First they covered ten kilometres or so, on foot, of course, because other facilities weren't available in those days, and people weren't afraid of walking fast and far. Then they climbed long slopes up to a kind of refuge perched aloft like an eagle's eyrie, where they spent a cheerful evening together by candlelight. Next morning they rose early and set off for the goal of their climb, equipped with hemp ropes and the stout nailed boots worn then, which struck showers of sparks from the rock in the dark. The party made good progress. But gradually the weather changed. The wind began to get up, and the sky to fill with clouds. This made the climbing slower and harder work. When the young men finally reached the summit, snowflakes were beginning to fall in icy whirlwinds. To them, however, success was what mattered, and they celebrated their victory with some triumphant yodelling. Now all they had to do was make the descent, not easy, since the rock was covered by verglas in places. Remember, this was a time when hardly anyone abseiled. The mountaineers had to climb down long passages, giving each other a hand, and when they finally arrived on the névé it was enveloped in mist.'

'Was it difficult terrain?'

'Yes. It wasn't very large, but they had to traverse it diagonally, and the tracks they'd made coming up had been covered by the wind, so they had difficulty in finding them. When at last they reached a moraine fifty or so metres above a little col they had crossed that morning, a gust of wind swept the clouds aside, and they saw Constanze standing in the middle of the col, calling Ulrich and signalling him to come. They all saw her, they recognized her, they were staggered. The wind was plastering her long peasant skirt against her stomach. She never stopped looking their way, making great beckoning gestures all the time. "Stanzi!" shouted Ulrich.

"She's crazy!" groaned my grandfather ... "She couldn't bear to be separated from her husband even for a day. Imagine coming all that way, in her condition!" "What a rash thing to do!" exclaimed one of the others. "We must go to her, help her back to the hut, make her rest, get back down ..." But the wind had already blown up more eddies of mist, and the col had disappeared from view. Ulrich was the first to start hurrying down the scree slope, stopping only to shout now and then, "Wait for me, Stanzi! Wait for me!" When he reached the col, however, there was no one there. His friends joined him, and they too were forced to confirm that the place was deserted.'

'Could the young woman have fallen?'

'Not really. There were certainly some scree slopes below the col, but they weren't very steep, and you couldn't have a bad fall there. Besides, there was a little track marking the route at that point. The young men turned in every direction, shouting: "Constanze! Constanze! Stanzi! We're here! Are you hurt? Hey, Constanze!" ... There was no reply. They climbed back up a little way and then began a thorough search of the area. By chance the mist lifted again so that they could see their surroundings. There really wasn't anyone there ... "She must have gone back down to the hut when she saw us," suggested one of them. "Then let's get there, quick!" replied another. They hurried down the path, still calling from time to time, but with no more success than before. Careering down the slopes, taking steep paths and short cuts, making the gravel fly beneath their feet, frantic with anxiety at the idea that Constanze had just gone all this way ahead at such speed they finally reached the hut. It was empty. They succumbed to deep dejection. Exhausted and overcome, they sank down on the primitive benches surrounding the pine table. Ulrich was pale and desperate. "I just don't understand! It's impossible!" said my grandfather. "We were all of us looking for her up there; we'd surely have found her if she'd been near the col... She isn't here either... and when she saw us, we couldn't have missed her if she'd climbed towards us!" '

'Did they search the hut area?'

'All round it, until nightfall. Well, they'd been walking and climbing for two days, but they were young and physically very fit, and Constanze couldn't have outdistanced them like that, particularly in her condition. They met in the cabin again around a candle when it had become too dark. There was none of the warmth and good fellowship of the previous evening. They were all tired, worried, tormented by the mystery that clung about Constanze's strange appearance and disappearance. Suddenly Ulrich rose, paler than ever. "I feel sure something's happened to Stanzi!" he muttered. "Not necessarily here... maybe down below... I don't know, but I want to go back down. I'm off!" "Not tonight! You're mad!" said my grandfather. "We're all worn out. We must rest for a few hours, we have to! We'll go back down with you tomorrow." "I'm going this evening! I must! I know the way, there will soon be a moon." "But it'll take you hours! Remember all that way we came up yesterday!" "I'll make it!" And he gathered up his things, fastened on his sack, buttoned up his cloth jacket, and set off alone into the night.'

'Didn't anyone go with him?'

'No. He made up his mind suddenly, and it was true that they were all very tired and saw no need to redescend in such haste. After all, Ulrich would find paths and mule tracks, and he would indeed soon have the moon to light him on his way. So they all gave themselves up to a few hours' rest, and then, in the morning, after another brief search in the vicinity of the hut, they too redescended. But when they reached the village a few hours later, they found it in deep mourning. Pretty Stanzi was dead. She'd gone into premature labour the night after Ulrich left, and had a haemorrhage which proved fatal. They hadn't been able to save the baby, which quickly followed its mother into death, and now the village was getting ready for a double funeral. So what they all saw could only have been the young woman's ghost, come to say a last farewell to her beloved husband. The sheer strength of their love had made this supernatural manifestation possible.'

And that, I may tell you, you, is a true story.

PASSION

Do you know who loved the high mountains more than anyone else ever did, idolized them even, to the extent of devoting his entire life, his actions, his thoughts, his every breath to them? Have you any idea who it was? I'll give you a thousand guesses!

No doubt you hesitate, with so many illustrious names, great deeds and famous climbing stories crowding into your mind.

Could it have been Horace-Bénédict de Saussure, the young Genevan who became so enamoured of the Alps in his twentieth year that his whole life took a new turn, culminating in his ardent quest for the summit of Mont Blanc? Was it one of the others who loved that mountain: Bourrit, Paccard, Balmat, or the valiant Henriette d'Angeville? Then again, what about Edward Whymper, first to climb the Aiguille Verte and the Matterhorn? Or his companion Michel Croz who lost his life so terribly in the course of the latter conquest?

Candidates for the title come thick and fast. Here's a whole bunch of them, all enthusiastic, spirited, afire with dreams: Preuss, Carrel, Coolidge, Guido Rey, Graham Brown, Moore, Forbes, Eccles, Cassin, Gervasutti, Lammer, Mummery, Young, Harrer, Heckmair, Lucien Devies, Tézenas du Montcel, Etienne Bruhl, Armand Charlet, Lachenal, Tensing, Lionel Terray, Joe Brown, Arturo Ottoz, Don Whillans, Walter Bonatti, Doug Scott, Reinhold Messner, Chris Bonington, John Harlin, Patrick Gabarrou, Mick Fowler, Jerzy Kukuczka?

They come in their hundreds, in their thousands, eyes shining with that reflection of the sky bestowed by high altitude on those who have approached it. Here they are, radiant, the wind in their hair, their tanned faces illuminated by smiles flashing white amidst the sunburn. Who among this great multitude knew and loved the mountains better than any of the rest?

What a strange question! . . . Still, it must surely be one of those people!

No, you're wrong! It was Vincent Colomine.

Who? you ask. Never heard of him! Nobody's ever come across his name! You must be joking! He's not in any book, yearbook, mountaineering magazine or Alpine journal, not in any anthology, or guide-book, or any account of the third solo winter ascent of a route on the flank of the satellite of some secondary gendarme. In short, his name isn't to be found anywhere!

So who may he have been, this man who loved the fabulous world we're conjuring up more than any the others? A Savoyard, perhaps? Some mediaeval chamois hunter? Some crystal collector of the heroic era?

No, you're still wide of the mark!

It is a very strange story. No one knows it, and perhaps you wouldn't believe it if I didn't tell you the whole thing from beginning to end.

Furthermore, it begins modestly and in a somewhat banal manner, for Vincent was born in very humble circumstances in Paris, in the quartier des Ternes: to be precise, in the rue Lebon, where his parents kept a small shop selling drapery and stationery under the sign of *La Bonne Renommée*.

It was in this shop and the first-floor flat above it that the child grew up, among the darning wools and cotton reels, the tailor's chalks and knitting needles, buttons and hat-pins, exercise books with squared paper and bottles of violet ink. If I add that the three colour prints on the walls of the little sitting room which was the centre of family life were of Millet's *Angelus*, Fragonard's *The Stolen Kiss* and the cliffs of Étretat, you will see how unpropitious this environment was to the subject which is our present concern.

Vincent remained an only son. His parents did their best to give him a good but not over-ambitious education. At that time, of course, the overriding aim of education was to teach children to read, write, spell and do sums. The rudiments of geography and history, civics and morality might at a pinch be thrown in. Such notions would now make whole generations of educational advisers and psychologists roar with derisive laughter ... I can't help it and nor can you. That's how it was.

No doubt Vincent Colomine preferred his electric train set and playing marbles to lessons, but he worked conscientiously and industriously, and bit by bit he acquired the knowledge then thought indispensable to plying a trade.

What else do you want know about him? Oh, you're thinking that he spent his holidays in the mountains? No such thing! ...Well, in the Jura, anyway? Or the Auvergne? ...No, you're still wrong! He used to go to stay with a family cousin, an old lady who had a small house in a village in Artois. It was here in this flat landscape, among kitchen gardens arranged in straight rows, among rabbits and chickens, that the child discovered there was something in the world besides the tarmac of the pavements in Paris and the Bois de Boulogne.

However, all his ideas were turned upside down one fine spring day, as the consequence of a phenomenon which passed unnoticed by many and was preceded by a very ordinary occurrence. Life sometimes does depend on coincidences or insignificant events.

That morning a lesson on Alpine geography had already struck a chord within the child. Under their schoolmaster's eye, the pupils had been reading aloud, one by one, paragraphs from a chapter about the Graian Alps and the Pennine Alps.

Some of them stumbled through their passages of text in a distinctly laborious manner. One such was Henri Jeulin, who began the reading:

'The Graian Alps (Alpes Graiæ, not to be transit ... translated as the Greek Alps) probably devire ... derive ... their name from a word in the Cel ... Cel ... '

'Celtic!' put in the teacher, drily.

'In the Celtic language ... *craig* ... mean ... meaning stone or peak. They extend from Mount Denis ...'

'Mount Cenis! Please concentrate, Jeulin!'

'Mount Cenis, or rather from the Roche-Melon ... Teeheehee! ... Melon!'

The other pupils roared with laughter.

'Kindly go on!'

'To the col of the ... Seigne and to Petit-Mont-Blanc, forming a kind of ... arc with its conex ... convex side turned in the direction of ... of Italy, which it separates from the department of ... of Savoie.'

The class was getting quietly bored, Vincent included. But he woke up a little later when they reached a passage read aloud by Ferret in a firm voice:

'This is the famous Mont Blanc massif, less complex and vast than that of Monte Rosa, but including the highest peak in the Alps and indeed in Europe, if we regard the Caucasus as part of Asia ...'

Vincent liked the picture this description conjured up.

And he was overwhelmed by the paragraph Téguise then read:

'There is just one way across the Mont Blanc massif, and it is a route only for the more daring tourist. "This is a marvellous place," writes Topffer, "for lovers of Alpine solitude, of fearsome peaks and formidable glaciers ... There are no roads, merely steep paths which should not be tackled without a guide. All who love free, unconstrained walking, poetry that is new and great spaces, silence, the mystery and the strange emotions aroused by vast and untamed nature, should go by way of the Allée-Blanche." '

Vincent Colomine listened with his mouth open. When his own turn came a little later, it was with emotion but in a clear voice that he continued the reading. At this point the text quoted one Francis Wey, who was equally eloquent:

' "The immensity of the spectacle, the steep, precipitous slope of the peaks falling away around you, the depths of the distance where the flattened line of the Jura can be seen beyond Lake Geneva; your isolated situation up in the air on this narrow platform; the chasms around you, the vast extent of the snow slopes, the brilliance with which they stand out against the glaucous translucence of the walls of ice; the sharp outline of the rocky crests, the great blue shadows they cast and the procession of bristling needles diminishing into the distance, all combine to fill you with admiration bordering on amazement." '

'Very good, Colomine!' said the teacher. 'Carry on, Belliard.'

And so a truly fascinating geography lesson continued. Arithmetic was next. Then everyone went home for lunch and came back in the afternoon for more lessons, and ordinary life would have claimed its dues again, had not something else entered Vincent's world at almost the same time.

His mother had asked him to call on an old lady who was a customer of hers after school, taking her a selection of tapestry wools which he had put in his satchel. He did his errand conscientiously, was rewarded for his trouble with a caramel, and came home as the setting sun was bathing the city in radiant light. And at the end of the Avenue de la Grande Armée, he saw a huge, swollen, superb and fantastic cloud. As I said before, very few people took any notice of it, but it captivated the boy.

It was the kind meteorologists call a cumulus cloud, a term which is both pedantic and very inadequate to describe something so splendid.

For Vincent saw a sight of extraordinary magnificence. Resting on the horizon, its white immensity spread and rose to assault the sky. It consisted of great luminous masses, deep ravines, blue-tinged cliffs, strange valleys, mysterious and fluffy chasms, rolling ridges fringed with gold, long snowy slopes piling up and up on each other, making for infinity, making for the azure sky.

Clouds are often blurred at the edges, but this one was brightly clear-cut, full and perfect, sumptuous ...

You could see shadowy gorges in it, valleys of dazzling clarity, dark and impassable precipices, silver lakes, softly undulating plateaux, gigantic mountain walls, supple and sinuous crests that seemed to be edged with gilt, and an impressive series of subsidiary peaks rising to the culminating dome which capped the edifice with an imperial crown.

The child thought he was looking at a mountain, a Himalayan peak of light. That morning's lesson came back to his mind. It was taking shape before his very eyes, both present here and immaterial.

Standing by the side of the avenue, eyes wide with wonder, Vincent could not tear himself away from the sight. He sought out paths and passages and imagined himself moving along them, over those slopes of bright vapour, climbing higher and higher, finally reaching the summit.

It was a riveting game. The cloud, in all its majesty, remained perfectly still and allowed the little boy to contemplate it as, holding his breath, he discovered the fascinating beauty of the high mountains. He remembered the sight for ever.

At last he had to tear himself away and go on home.

'What sort of time is this to come in?' enquired his mother tartly.

But the die was cast. Vincent thought only of the heights. He patiently started collecting anything to do with the Alps: cigarette cards, pictures on Nestlé chocolate wrappers, postcards, articles cut from the magazines his father threw away, and in the end a few books ... His treasure grew, and his passion remained intact. One day, he knew, one day he would go and see the mountains of which he dreamed, but he was too young yet.

Two years later, he thought the moment had come at last.

The elderly cousin in Artois had a bad attack of flu and died in the winter. Consequently, the Colomines were planning to go away somewhere else with their son for two weeks' holiday next summer. They earnestly discussed their destination over meals, as if it were a great adventure. A lady who was one of their customers had suggested Dieppe, another Vichy, another La Bérarde ...

La Bérarde! By now the boy had the geography of the Alps at his fingertips. Would he see the mountains for the first time at La Bérarde? Would he get a chance to see the Meije?

He was afraid of influencing his parents' decision the wrong way if he spoke up.

'Vichy would be good for your liver!' Madame Colomine told her husband.

'There's nothing the matter with my liver, thank you,' he replied. 'I'm inclined to favour La Bérarde myself.'

'But I'm afraid it would be cold in the mountains, and it can't be much fun having things blocking your view the whole time.'

Instantly and with a shudder, all in a flash, Vincent realized that the wonderful journey of discovery he hoped to make could be ruined by a constant flow of disappointed, down-to-earth comments: "I told you it would be cold!' 'I really don't care for all those peaks blocking the view!' 'We should have gone to Vichy!' . . . No, it was impossible! Such a thing was out of the question! Everything must be perfect when he first set eyes on his mountains.

Suddenly he made his decision. In its way, it was a heroic one.

'I'd like to go to Dieppe,' he begged. 'To see ships and the sea. I could look for shells and go fishing with Daddy . . . and Mummy could rest on the beach . . .'

His arguments won the day, reconciling the two factions. And so the blessed moment when he would finally encounter the object of his distant passion was preserved in all its purity. It must come in circumstances ensuring that nothing marred its beauty.

His parents liked Dieppe. The family went back there several years running. Vincent, now a young man, was still possessed by his love for the mountains.

His collection, to which he grew more attached than ever, now contained a hundred or so books which he had read with intense interest. He liked some better than others, but they had all added to his knowledge of the topography and history of the object of his devotion. He was quietly on the way to becoming a specialist.

Since he was working hard at school, his father was persuaded to let him stay on after the first public exam and study for his baccalauréat, which he passed easily. But the ambitions of the Colomine parents stopped there, and he had to choose a trade. As the stationery and drapery business did not interest him at all, it was natural enough for him to say he would like to be a bookshop assistant, and he enjoyed the job.

Several more years went by. Vincent had his independence now, but he was overcome by great diffidence when he thought of seeing the mountains themselves and how to set about it: venturing to start out, to see with his own eyes the resplendent wonders whose essence he had perceived and grasped that day, their marvels subsequently confirmed by innumerable accounts in the pages of his library, by the intensive study of maps, by the pictures in his books, so that he could now recognize any mountain face, any Aiguille or any peak at a glance.

The walls of his lodgings, where he never let anyone else come, were covered with superb photographs of the Matterhorn seen from the Lac Noir, the summit ridge of Mont Blanc, the procession of the Eiger, the Mönch and the Jungfrau, the Grand Combin and the Gran Paradiso, which seemed to him like that first vision he had been granted of his fabulous mountains.

He spent hours wondering where best to see them in actual fact. Should he approach gradually, or choose a face-to-face encounter? Should it be in Zermatt or Chamonix? And at what season?

But the gesture he had made in his youth, holding back when Fate, in the natural course of events, offered fulfilment, had endowed the whole business with new gravity. Every day, the act of embarking on the great adventure of an actual encounter at any one time rather than another struck him as increasingly audacious.

Apart from his grand passion, Vincent was a very ordinary young man. He was more athletic than might have been expected from his sedentary and intellectual way of life; he went for long walks or bicycle rides every Sunday, usually on his own. He particularly liked the woods and would sometimes spend the night there, lying at the foot of a tree in his sleeping bag and enjoying the dawn chorus.

He did not marry, partly out of timidity, partly for lack of suitable opportunities, and partly because he feared the necessary close relationship and a possible conflict between his two loves, as they would be, one of them inevitably tending to overcome the other. And he needed his feelings for the mountains to remain absolute. He regretted the lack of a child more than the lack of a wife. But he consoled himself with his dreams.

This is impossible, you will tell me. Impossible? All through the long, grey urban winters, isn't a real mountaineer possessed by the prospect of another season with all its fascinating routes? Doesn't he spend more time thinking of them, anticipating future climbs, preparing for them and imagining them than actually climbing in the strict sense of the word, particularly at high altitudes? So what's the difference?

Ah, you will reply, but such a mountaineer has already seen the mountains he's thinking of: he has experience of them ... yes, very well, he's seen them, but the mountains in his mind aren't always those he knows. He's just as interested in the new mountains he would like to climb, if not more so. If he's been climbing in Oisans, and is reasonably adventurous, doesn't he dwell with pleasure on the potential of the sheer walls of the Dolomites, the north faces of the Oberland, the clear glaciers of the Engadine? It was just the same for Vincent Colomine, except that not having seen anything at all yet, he dreamed all the more.

You can love from afar, in the absolute. And that is what he was content to do. He loved the mountains more than anything else. He adored them; he was crazy about them. He didn't absolutely have to see them with his own eyes, touch them, gain physical experience of them, feel tangible pleasures ... This attitude of his was akin to virginity. To know the mountains existed was enough to make him happy; that in itself was sufficiently wonderful.

The time came when the Colomine parents grew old and needed their son's care, ruling out any travel plans for many years. When they were dead he sold their shop and bought a small bookshop of his own in the Buttes Chaumont, with works both new and second-hand and a section devoted to mountaineering. He also lent books out, and had a number of faithful customers. Those with an interest in the Alps were particular favourites of his, but he dared not confide his secret passion to any of them.

He watched his old friends the clouds, particularly during his solitary expeditions. Sometimes they were strangers to his world. There were fluffy clouds of cotton wool, mists teased out in the air, untidy swirls of vapour, satin stitch in mother-of-pearl, long trails of soot on a turquoise ground, silver ships with all sails set, dark and menacing fortresses, shining icebergs, pearly lace, shoals of mauve fish, purple zebra stripes, infinite expanses of doves' wings, opalescent cameos, scattered archipelagos, white schooners, flares of gold, surf, waves, swelling seas ...

And sometimes they were like the wonderful cloud of his childhood. Then his heart would beat with emotion and desire, but all the same, he never again saw any architectural formation, however perfect, which could compare with the great pyramid of cupolas, the cathedral of light, he had seen on that first day.

The more time passed, the less did he feel brave enough to face the reality. He read that the mountains were changing. Property developers, ski-lift builders, the municipalites themselves, caring nothing for so much beauty, were exploiting sites for all they were worth. Money was winning out over any other values. There were tangles of pylons and cables everywhere, motorways and car parks, concrete and yet more concrete ... It hurt him. He would have liked to see his distant beloved earlier, in all her original purity.

Suppose he went and was disappointed? Had they managed to disfigure the object of his passion? He could not make up his mind to go.

He went, none the less, almost on the spur of the moment.

The years had already turned Vincent's hair white. His shoulders were stooped, his skin withered, but in his eyes, now pale, the light of his unrequited love still burned.

He had just sold his shop, and he feared the boredom of the solitary retirement ahead of him. Retirement, the antechamber to death ...

Then, one day in March, he met a former customer who told him she was going on holiday to Cordon, opposite the Mont Blanc range.

It's so simple, he told himself. Buy a train ticket and go. Something he had never ventured to do!

'You must tell me what it was like,' he asked her, suddenly full of a growing regret for spending his life so far from what should have been its centre. 'Or no, wait, send me a postcard! I'll be expecting it. I'll look forward to it.'

No doubt touched by the old bookseller's request, his customer remembered him and sent the postcard he asked for. There were plenty like it in his files, but this one, written only the day before, was like a breath of fresh air blowing in on him. It showed the vast, extensive view of the whole mountain range from the Aiguille du Chardonnet to the Dômes de Miage, omnipresent and unreal, light and majestic.

This was the moment! It was now or never. Vincent would not venture too far into the mountains themselves, but he would go there and see the Promised Land, if only from a distance.

That very evening he caught a train to Sallanches.

He arrived in a fine drizzle of rain, which did not surprise him. He had already waited so long that it was nothing to wait a little longer, only a very little ... Besides, they were forecasting fine weather for next day. Vincent took a room with a view in a small hotel.

In the afternoon, when the rain had stopped, he went for a walk. The high mountains were still enveloped in cloud, but he could already taste the intense flavour of the hilly country landscape here.

Cordon was in between winter and spring. The snow had melted, but nature still seemed half dead, and the trees had no leaves. Only the dark pines rose here and there, bringing a note of sombre colour into the landscape. Apart from that you could see nothing but bare wood, leafless twigs and branches.

When you looked more closely, however, there were many signs of renewal. Little spring flowers were opening, huddling low in pastures scorched by frost – wild crocuses, white and purple, and pale yellow primroses while tufts of notched dandelion leaves were beginning to show among the grass, already putting out a timid bud or so on sheltered slopes.

Catkins hung from the bushes by the roadsides. The birds, forgetting the hard winter, were already uttering cheerful cheeps and twitters, and the tits, hopping from branch to branch, hovered to peck at seeds and then flew happily away.

You could hear the splashing of limpid little streams, and the clear sound of water constantly flowing into a stone trough. The wind and cold were a reminder of the recent wintry season. Pencils of sunlight piercing the clouds now and then heralded the coming of spring, while last autumn's dead, grey fallen leaves still whirled in a dry dance on the road.

His heart full of childlike joy, Vincent Colomine went back to his hotel, dazzled in advance by the wonders to come tomorrow. He dined on a fondue, feeling a secret jubilation. He was here! He was here at last! Life was opening up before him . . .

It was not life opening up . . . or was it, after all? He died of a stroke in the night.

When the mountains he had loved more than anyone showed themselves framed at his window, haloed in splendour, the rays of the sun fell only on a body which seemed to have fallen asleep, and a face with its features happy and relaxed.

What need I add to this story?

Events followed their due course. The hotel proprietor notified the police, who found papers and an address. As there was no family, and there were no precise instructions for a funeral, Vincent Colomine was buried in a public grave in the little cemetery of Cordon, facing the Mont Blanc range, under the protecting shadow of the baroque church, whose onion dome was covered with fine, shining scales which reflected the light of the sun.

He was one with his mountains for ever.

THE VETERAN

The two climbers emerged on the crest, greeted by a violent gust of wind and a flurry of spindrift. Maurice Troènaz, the guide, immediately began to shorten the rope, making several coils which he slid over his rucksack, whilst Léon Puidoux, his client, sitting back on his heels, lost himself in contemplation of the slopes of the North Face of the Gran Paradiso which the two had just climbed together.

One hour later the two men reached the summit of the Gran Paradiso, a long rocky belvedere flanked by curious turrets, which rears up like a vessel's prow between the valleys of Cogne and Valsavaranche. Clouds filled the low-lying plains, and only the snowy mountain ranges rose up into the sun, like golden islands floating on a sea of luminous vapour.

A statue of the Virgin crowns the summit. The pair settled down on a large stony platform nearby.

'There's nothing to the descent!' said Maurice, reassuringly. 'A beginner in Class 6 could do it, on skis. It's a glorious day, and we're not in any hurry now. Take as many photos as you like. But let's have a bite first. It's nearly eleven hours since we left the hut, though it may not feel like it, and we've had practically nothing to eat. All the same, I'd have expected better conditions at this time of year. But we've done well, and it's not too late.'

'That last six ropelengths on hard ice, where you had to cut steps all the way,' replied Monsieur Puidoux, 'I don't think I've come across any ice like that since the North Face of the Ebnefluh. Have some sausage? Here, let me give you a piece of bread. Where's the thermos? ...Sorry, I'll have a quick sip first; my throat's like blotting-paper. Whew, that's better! Here, your turn! And the belays weren't too great, either, with all the ice you kept knocking down on me. Cold, too ... my finger-tips went completely numb, which rarely happens to me. My hands were quite dead by the time I came to remove the belay screws and move on. Where's that cheese got to? I'm sure there's a bit left ... ah, here it is. Want some? The séracs were solid, and we were lucky to find those ribs of hard snow the whole way up the first part. We lost a lot of time at that second bergschrund. I really enjoyed it! A good climb, excellent!'

All the parties which had come up by the normal route had already got to the top and gone down again. All except one, which at last slowly reached the crest and forced its way across the rocky outcrops on the summit ridge. The leader was Franco Revel, a Courmayeur guide whom Troènaz knew well, and whom he had greeted the evening before, at the hut. His client was at the end of his tether. He was a tall, clean-shaven old man whose white hair fluttered in the mountain wind. His face bore the signs of exhaustion. He let himself sink to the ground by the side of the statue and, resting his head against it, shut his eyes and tried to get his breath back. Revel took a thermos flask from his rucksack and made him drink a mug of hot liquid.

'*Va bene!*' said the tourist. '*Ho bisogno solamente di riposarmi un poco ... Non preoccuparti!*'

The guide did his best to wedge him firmly, using his rucksack and, unroping, he went to join the others who were a few metres away, giving them a meaning look.

'What's the matter with him?' asked Troènaz.

'Nothing except old age!' sighed Franco, lighting a cigarette. 'Old age and the obstinacy of a mule. He's one of my clients from Milan, he's been climbing with me for a long time. But he's not up to it any more, he's past it! To think he wants to do Mont Blanc again, at seventy! What a hope! It's quite something that he got as far as this. But he reckons this is just a training climb. Once we're down I'm going to have a tough job getting him to admit he has to give up the high mountains. And other climbing too, most likely. You can see how he feels. Mountains were his life; he doesn't have many other interests. His wife died young, his children aren't very pleasant to him, and he owns a small factory which is causing him anxiety. It'll be a terrible wrench for him, giving up the mountains. Still ... there's a time for everything, isn't there?'

'Sure!' replied Maurice Troènaz.

'Well, good to have seen you again!' said Revel, throwing away his fag-end. 'I'd better go back to the old boy. We're not down yet. See you at the Guides' Festival on 15th August. I'll be coming with the Courmayeur delegation. We'll have a couple of jars! 'Bye, Maurice!'

'See you, Franco! Good luck for the descent!'

Monsieur Puidoux had been listening to the conversation without saying a word. From time to time he glanced at the statue and the elderly, dried-up figure leaning against it. He went on automatically chewing bread and slices of sausage, without going over the memories of the recent climb as he normally did.

Suddenly, sounding somewhat portentous, he called to his guide.

'Maurice!' he said. 'I want you to make me a solemn promise.'

Troènaz stared at him in surprise, about to laugh, but Léon Puidoux's expression was grave.

'I'm not joking, Maurice. I'm going to ask you to swear an oath. You must swear you will never let me get like that ... that ...

He hesitated for a moment, searching for words.

'That old wreck,' he finally went on. 'That bit of human scrap ... that caricature of a mountaineer. Never let me get to be such a shadow of myself ... Never let me labour up easy slopes, panting, because I didn't know when to stop climbing ... I'm sure this poor fellow has no idea what's happened to him, or he'd feel ashamed. As for what that Italian guide said, it's true: there really is a time for everything, and you have to be able to admit it, have the sense to stop in time. So this is what I'm asking you, Maurice: I'm asking you to tell me the truth before I reach that stage. Mind you, I'm pretty sure I'll notice for myself, but you never know, it may come on imperceptibly. And I want to go out honourably, before I get like ... like him!'

'But you're miles away from that!' exclaimed Maurice. 'You've just done the North Face of the Gran Paradiso in fine style. A youngster couldn't have done it better. Sure on your feet, sound in wind and limb, the lot! Hell, it's a real pleasure to see you cramponning! How old are you, anyway? Fifty-six? Fifty-seven? OK, fifty-seven! You've got many good years ahead of you. And good climbs, too!'

Léon Puidoux's face lit up. Of course, he knew perfectly well he'd been climbing like a youngster this morning. But even if you stay healthy and fit, you can't ignore the stealthy accumulation of the years, the verdict of successive calendars, the poignant approach of the final reckoning. Léon Puidoux frequently thought about it. It seemed to him only yesterday that he'd celebrated his fiftieth birthday with a good party, and so as to have the company of all his friends he'd even paid for Maurice to come along with his father, Auguste Troènaz, who had been his first guide, was now retired, and to tell the truth was hardly older than Puidoux himself.

'Of course I know it's not going to be immediately,' he said. 'Moreover, I can say that so far as I'm concerned everything's fine. I get on very well with my wife, she's always right behind me, and with my three sons, not to mention my wonderful granddaughter. My professional work is satisfying too. And though I won't claim I'd say goodbye to the mountains with a light heart, I believe I'll be able to accept it when the time comes, and there'll be many other things to interest me in life, thank

God! But I am absolutely determined never to make such a spectacle of myself as that poor pig-headed old man we've just met. So Maurice, that's why I'm asking you – asking you most earnestly – to swear you'll tell me the moment you see me showing real signs of decline, just in case I don't notice myself.'

'But, look here . . .' objected Maurice, embarrassed.

'Sorry, I must insist!' went on Léon Puidoux. 'I beg you. It's a service I'm asking you to do me, as a friend, and it means a lot to me. Promise, or I shall feel this beautiful day has been spoilt!'

'O.K. – don't worry. If it means so much to you, then I give you my word,' agreed Maurice Troènaz. 'But I don't expect to have to keep my promise in a hurry, I can tell you!'

Léon Puidoux smiled happily. Relieved of his anxiety, he now wanted nothing but to revel in the sense of contentment induced by this latest climb, this additional north face, this new summit. He amused himself by identifying the peaks and ranges which rose up from the blanket of cloud, pulled out his old Rollei to click away at the landscape, and when, wanting to be photographed himself, he gave the camera to Maurice, the latter had to suppress a little smile when he noticed the effort his client was making to stand up straight and saw him smooth several strands of hair over his balding brow with an apparently casual gesture.

A few moments later, on the descent, Troènaz's rope caught up with Franco Revel's. Revel's client, clearly exhausted, was moving like an automaton, taking small and cautious steps. Léon Puidoux lengthened his stride to overtake him, even though the snow was already deep and soft away from the track.

'At this rate they won't get to the hut before evening,' he muttered, for the benefit of his guide.

Maurice Troènaz had been right in assuring Monsieur Puidoux that his fitness and experience would allow him to go on climbing for many more years. In following seasons their partnership was successful in making some very fine expeditions which included the Route Major, the East Ridge of the Crocodile, the Pilier Cordier, the Dent Blanche and the South Face of the Meije. Monsieur Puidoux trained regularly during the year and, when he arrived in Chamonix, he was almost ready to attack big climbs straight away. He had only a very slight tendency to harp on the fact that he was not feeling the ravages of age.

'I feel really on form these days!' he would announce. 'I hope it doesn't sound boastful, but I don't see myself growing old. This winter I went cycling every Sunday. My sons don't do as much. And at Fontainebleau I can still do the same circuits, and even occasionally a new problem. I feel really young, and that's a fact. Do you know, Maurice, if the light's good I can still read *Le Monde* without glasses!'

Maurice Troènaz, who had no intention of reading *Le Monde*, with or without glasses, nevertheless greeted the announcement of this feat deferentially.

'And you won't forget your promise, will you?' Léon Puidoux reminded him from time to time, usually when they had returned from a good climb. 'You know what I mean! The promise you made on the Gran Paradiso, to warn me when I start going downhill.'

And his guide would invariably and obligingly reply, 'Well, that won't happen in a hurry!'

Several years went by in this fashion until one day, quite suddenly, after a week's holiday during which they had already successfully done two good routes, a phone call summoned Léon Puidoux back to Paris on business. He was disconsolate.

'We'll meet again next year!' he declared. 'And at any rate it'll give me the chance to do plenty of skiing this winter. I'm just thinking, though … maybe we could get round to doing the Chamonix/Zermatt traverse we've talked about so much during our last week? I've never managed to find time for it yet.'

Unfortunately, a nasty fall off-piste at Val-d'Isère led to yet another postponement of this plan. Léon Puidoux had injured his right knee. There was talk of an operation, and then they tried electrical treatment, to avoid too long a period of immobilization. The knee did not mend well. In May surgery became inevitable, and there could be no question of planning a season's climbing in the summer. Monsieur Puidoux took the opportunity to spend his holidays in the Midi with all his family, but he missed the mountains so much that he went to Chamonix for three days in August to see the Aiguilles again, contact his guide and make plans for next year. He was still walking with a stick but, rested, relaxed and sunburnt, he appeared full of energy. He invited Troènaz to dinner at the Hotel Eden and regaled him at length with his tales of knee-caps and menisci.

'Just one of those accidents bound to happen to a sportsman!' he declared cheerfully. 'In spite of all the time I've had to spend flat on my back, I haven't put on an ounce! I was even able to take an old pair of flannel bags I've had since I was young to the Midi with me. Not an ounce! I've never felt so fit in my life!'

All the same, next summer Maurice saw that Léon Puidoux had changed. A year's stressful work had left him tired. His firm was facing a multitude of problems. The accounts did not balance, and foreign companies, being more competitive, got the contracts. There was talk of laying off some of the staff. Throughout the year Léon Puidoux had to battle on in difficult conditions, taking home his files in the evenings and over the weekend, and he had almost no time for training. On top of this, the unexpected interruption caused by his accident had somewhat lowered his spirits. His face was gaunt, his hair thinning, and it was evident that he found the mountains harder going than before. On the other hand, he no longer breathed a word about the promise. Maurice sought patiently to reacclimatize him, but the results did not live up to his hopes.

'Perhaps it'll be better next summer!' he thought to himself.

But he was never able to tell, because the season was a wash-out. A few climbs in the Aiguilles Rouges and on the Rocher de Leschaux – that was all the two of them managed to snatch from the appalling weather. Once again, major projects had to be postponed for a year.

Eventually they met again the following summer, round the table at the Argentière Hut. Their first climb, to get the legs moving again, was to be the traverse of the Tour Noir, but Maurice Troènaz scrutinized his client with concern. This time the change in him was profound, so much so that the short descent from the Grands Montets téléphérique to the glacier had already tired him out. His heavy lids and the dark marks under his eyes made circles of wrinkles round them, and the beginnings of a double chin showed here and there. His nose seemed pinched, his gaze remained fixed, and a nervous tic made him continually stroke his lips with his fingers, as if he wanted to wipe them. He drank his soup with little noisy gulps, hardly speaking at all, totally preoccupied with himself and with his weariness.

'We'll see how it goes tomorrow,' said Maurice to himself philosophically.

They did indeed. Monsieur Puidoux found innumerable excuses for his slowness. He was no longer used to his boots, which were hurting him. One crampon was too tight and had to be loosened. The rope was over-long, so that he had to hold too many coils. But when the gap had been reduced, the rope turned out to be too short, and didn't allow him to move with his accustomed rhythm. A number of such excuses were proffered, all the way up to the col. And when, on the summit, Maurice Troènaz suggested abandoning the traverse and going down by the ordinary route, he encountered little opposition.

'Maybe you're right, Maurice!' agreed Monsieur Puidoux. 'I can see some clouds which seem to bode no good.'

During the long descent to Lognan which followed, the guide continued to watch his client, and he remembered his promise. What a stupid commitment to have taken on! What an embarrassing mission, far beyond the bounds of his responsibilities! At the same time, he had to admit that Monsieur Puidoux might have been very wise to take such a precaution, for he was evidently unaware of his own condition, and once in the cable-car he immediately began constructing wholly impossible projects. Maurice Troènaz replied evasively and decided to broach the tricky subject as soon as possible. But of course it couldn't be done in the cabin. Nor in the evening, when he was off duty and they met again at the Guides' Bureau. It wasn't something you could very well mention in public. However, having taken his decision Maurice did not want to delay, so he invited his client to have a drink at Mélanie's.

'It's on me!' he insisted. 'There's something I have to tell you.'

It wasn't easy. Léon Puidoux seemed to be doing his best to keep the talk to impersonal subjects such as the accident in the Mont Blanc tunnel, last winter's hurricane, the problems of car-parking ...

Maurice interrupted him abruptly. 'Monsieur Puidoux! You remember the North Face of the Gran Paradiso?'

'Do I remember? Ah – do I remember ... I think I could describe every detail of that pitch where ... '

'That's not it, Monsieur Puidoux. I want to talk about the summit, that time when the old Italian arrived utterly knackered. You wrung a promise out of me then. Okay, this is what I have to tell you now, and believe me, I don't enjoy it. But I do think that, if you don't want to see yourself deteriorating, it's time you stopped climbing.'

'You must be out of your mind, Maurice!' Léon Puidoux snapped. 'Surely you're not going to pass sentence on me after our very first climb, and after such a long, tedious interval ... an unintentional one, as you very well know. My work, my knee, the filthy weather, they all played a part. Now I'm starting again in earnest, and we'll see what we will see! Right, so now I've made that clear, yes, of course I remember the promise I made you give me. And I stick to it, in principle. But I'm amazed, and quite rightly, I really am amazed to find you jumping at the first chance to remind me of it, in such an inopportune way. Unless of course you mean you don't want to climb with me any more and other clients have been monopolizing you over these last few years. In which case, you might have picked some other way of letting me know ...'

'No, no, that's not it at all!' stammered Maurice, disconcerted.

'Then we'll forget it' proclaimed Léon Puidoux, in ringing tones. 'You're young, but that's no reason to see me as a relic of mountaineering prehistory. I feel fine, and no matter what you're implying, there aren't many men of my age to equal me, not many at all.'

'But I never said ...'

'Maybe not in so many words, but it comes to the same thing. I know what other people are like, and I know myself. I'm glad to say it's not time for me to beat a retreat yet. And please note that when it *is* time, I'll be able to see it myself, with the clarity of vision I believe I've always shown. In the meantime, I don't think we need to recall the Gran Paradiso. I hope I've made myself quite clear?'

'You certainly have, Monsieur Puidoux!' Maurice agreed.

'Then let's talk about our plans instead,' his client went on, mollified. 'I grant you, I do need a bit more training than usual. The rocks are snowed up, but that gives us a chance to do some of the routes I've always dreamt about. The Younggrat, for example. I won't suggest the Welzenbach route, also on the Breithorn – you see, I'm being very sensible. On the other hand the Biancograt, on the Piz Bernina, seems a perfectly feasible idea. And then there's the Sentinelle Rouge. I've never yet had any luck there yet. And ...'

Maurice Troènaz listened, feeling depressed. He had tried to speak out, and had obviously got nowhere. What more could he do? He steered the discussion towards the subject of training climbs. Once again, Monsieur Puidoux reacted as if he were in the prime of life.

'The North-East Face of the Courtes? The North Buttress of the Chardonnet?'

They finally agreed, with some hesitation on both sides, on the Rochefort Ridge. Léon Puidoux found this project too modest, whilst Maurice Troénaz thought it too ambitious, and it was he who was proved right in the end – they had to turn back at the foot of the Dent du Géant, having lost far too much time. They tried two other routes without any greater success. Monsieur Puidoux was in a bad temper, kept finding good reasons to explain his lack of form, and complained – although not being successful in getting up anything – of not moving on to harder things. And so the pair found themselves, one fine evening, at the Couvercle Hut, where Maurice recognised Franco Revel at another table and hurried over to greet him.

'Come and have a quick word,' he said. 'I want to ask you a question.'

And when they had moved away from the crowded tables, he said: 'I've been thinking about you lately. I was wondering what happened to your client, the one on the Gran Paradiso. You remember, the day you were with that old man who didn't want to pack it in.'

'You bet I remember!' replied Revel. 'Poor old boy, I guess he must be dead. Anyway, he doesn't write to me any more. It was a tough job, getting him to see he had to call it a day.'

'Exactly!' Maurice persisted. 'Just how did you do it? You see, I've got the same problem. We'd done the North Face that day on the Gran Paradiso. Well, up on the summit, when my client saw yours, he made me promise never to let him get to that point. And now he's not far from it, I just can't make him understand.'

'You told him, then?' Franco asked, with some interest.

'Yes, I told him. He made me promise, after all.'

And Troènaz described what he had done in detail.

'You used words to tell him,' said Franco. 'Now you must try another way, without words.'

'So how do you expect me to tell him except in words?'

'Another way, I said. Or rather, the mountain must tell him. How did you react to his plans?'

'Well, I'm doing my best to make him slow down, show him he can't do these things any more.'

'And he objects, right?'

'You've said it, he most certainly does object! There's no end to the argument! But he just isn't up to it any more, even on the easy routes. And he's not happy about it, either.'

'Well, you can at least make him happy!' suggested Franco. 'Go along with his suggestions and then, like I said, the mountain will do the job itself. It may be a harder way in the end, but I can't see any other.'

'I guess you're right,' Maurice decided.

Next day, Monsieur Puidoux walked for only an hour, towards the Pointe Isabelle. The slopes seemed tedious to him, leading to a boring objective which didn't even provide a genuine high-altitude training.

'But what would you have preferred?' Troènaz asked, once they were back in the valley.

'Oh, I don't really know ... something different, anything! A real training climb up to 4000 metres, before tackling the serious stuff. Never mind these hills with their cattle pastures where you're getting me into training – why don't we try a big one, Monte Rosa, say? And once I'm used to the altitude again, then depending on the conditions I'm thinking of a route like the Biancograt, or maybe the Zmutt ridge. And after that ...'

'Right!' replied Maurice. 'We'll leave for Zermatt tomorrow, if you like, and do Monte Rosa. Whatever you say. I want you to enjoy yourself.'

Surprised by his rapid victory, Léon Puidoux displayed no wild enthusiasm. 'You've certainly taken your time to get the idea,' he remarked tersely.

Maurice Troènaz prepared the climb with care. If the mountain was to speak, as Revel had said it would, he might as well try to smooth the rough side of its tongue. The message was likely to be outspoken anyway. Besides, more than one such occasion might be needed to drive the point home. Maurice had made up his mind that for his part he would display the utmost patience.

They could not leave as soon as they had intended, since they had to wait for a depression accompanied by frequent downpours to pass over, so Monsieur Puidoux felt quite rested when the two men reached Zermatt. He was in a very talkative mood. The Bétemps Hut, two hours away from Rotenboden station, took the two of them in along with quite a number of other people intending to do the climb. A positively military discipline reigned in the hut: those climbers who were aiming for the North Face of the Lyskamm, and wanted to leave before the Monte Rosa mob, found themselves put firmly in their place departure time was the same for everybody, and the warden made a point of locking the door for the night. Troènaz felt sorry: he would gladly have joined the Lyskamm climbers to get a a head start and gain time in the morning.

Sure enough, next morning Monsieur Puidoux and his guide very soon found themselves at the tail end of the procession strung out on the slopes and, although they were not the only ones to be slow, they kept on losing ground. Maurice was determined to remain entirely passive. Too bad if they were outstripped by all and sundry. They went at Monsieur Puidoux's pace, stopped whenever he wanted to stop, started again only when he said he was ready to start, and – above all – there was no looking at watches. They were going to take their time, all the time they wanted ...

The highest point of Monte Rosa has an altitude of 4634 metres, but the Bétemps Hut is only at 2800 metres, so you have to climb a height difference of over eighteen hundred metres, along interminable snow-slopes. There are no appreciable technical difficulties, except for a few enormous crevasses which have to be circumvented or crossed on snow bridges. Otherwise, it's just a matter of following the deep track which leads to the summit in some six or seven hours, at a normal walking pace.

But when the first parties were beginning to come down on the way back, Maurice Troènaz and Léon Puidoux were only half-way up. Sitting on his rucksack, Monsieur Puidoux pretended not to notice them. He was absorbed in straightening out a crampon strap, and seemed to pay no attention to the comings and goings on the mountain.

'Shall we go?' Maurice finally asked.

They went, taking small steps. The Swiss guides returning to the hut glanced, with some surprise, at the Chamonix guide lagging so far behind, but there you are – these French make out they can do anything, and then they take all day for Monte Rosa, where you don't often see them anyway, busy as they are pottering about near the cable-cars ... As for Léon Puidoux, he was slightly surprised that, contrary to his usual custom, his guide did not urge him on, or indeed decide that, at this late hour, it was time to pack it in. Not at all! Troènaz seemed quite resigned to the long haul and was most attentive. He had only to carry on. Since for once he'd got his way over the choice of route, Léon Puidoux wasn't going to have it all end in failure. It would just take a bit of time, that's all. He was going to show that he was up to it. But he didn't feel too good. His heart seemed to be beating in his throat. Every five or six paces he felt so breathless that he had a short fit of dry coughing. And there seemed to be two little dazzling, luminous ventilators at the back of his eyes, clouding his vision.

There was no denying that this climb was becoming a real torment. The crevasses were opening up, and the snow bridges were no longer very firm. One of them, a kind of yellowish plug, split in the middle, made Monsieur Puidoux freeze in his tracks.

'I managed to get across it, and I've got you on a tight rope,' urged Maurice. 'Come on, then! We're lucky the bridge is still here at this time of day, after all those hordes have trampled across.'

They had reached 4000 metres, and it was already half past ten. Bright clouds were drifting in a dark blue sky, but there was not the slightest breath of wind and the heat was intense.

'I feel so hot!' sighed Léon Puidoux.

'Well, if the wind was blowing, as it often is up here, you'd be complaining of the cold! You know what the mountains are like.'

'I feel hot!' repeated Léon Puidoux.

They took four hours to get up the last six hundred metres, frequently stopping for a rest. The ridge at the end, studded with rocks, cost the old man a quite disproportionate effort. Troènaz said nothing and showed exceptional forbearance. He did not say a word about the way time was getting on, and just kept a bit of tension on the rope to help his client make progress.

On the summit Monsieur Puidoux collapsed on his rucksack. The guide had trouble making him drink and suck a few sweets.

'I think the mountains are changing,' muttered the old man, as if to excuse himself. 'It must be the extra glaciation, or maybe there's less glaciation.'

'That's right,' said Maurice. 'The mountains are changing, the crevasses have got deeper and the slopes even steeper since last time. And I don't know if you've noticed, but the days aren't the same as they used to be either, probably because of summer time. It's nearly half past two. Makes you wonder where the time has gone! We're the only ones who don't change, see? Here, make a bit of an effort, try to eat that marzipan bar!'

'Leave me alone, Maurice!' begged Monsieur Puidoux. 'I'm really not hungry. I just need some rest.'

'Well, you've done Monte Rosa now!' continued Maurice, who was afraid that the old man might fall asleep. 'You were right, after all. And now we must think about the Biancograt ...'

But Monsieur Puidoux was hardly listening. He was thinking that he still had to go back down those endless snow slopes he had just toiled up, and the prospect was shattering. For a moment he dreamt of a helicopter ... suppose he could be picked up here! He'd be willing to pay all that was required, and more ... But how could he let them know down below? How could he even admit it to Maurice? It would be the most abject surrender imaginable. No, he knew very well that he had to make the descent on foot, cost what it might.

It was an immense effort just to stand up. But he managed it and, firmly held on a tight rope by Maurice, who remained amazingly calm, he tackled the start of the descent step by step, move by move, his legs seeming to tuck into his body. So many folds and ridges in the ground, slopes, hollows, detours, crevasses to be skirted or jumped. When they reached the one which had given them so much trouble on the way up, the bridge had collapsed and they would have to make a considerable leap to get across.

'I can't do that!' said the old man.

'Of course you can!' replied Maurice. 'And to prove it, you're going to. I'll be holding you!'

'No, it's much too wide . . . it's quite impossible. Isn't there some way round? Surely there must be.'

'Well, just look at it! You can't see either end. And this still looks the likeliest spot. You'll land right in the middle of the track. Come on, let's get moving. Any idea how late it is? We've jumped plenty of other crevasses together, crevasses just like this one.'

'I can't do it!' Monsieur Puidoux insisted.

In the end Maurice jumped first and threatened to pull on the rope. His elderly client, apprehensive and clumsy, finally took off and crash-landed on the other side in a motionless little heap. In alarm, the guide hastened to bend over him, but there was nothing the matter except fear, exhaustion and shame.

Troènaz could not help giving his companion a bit of a shove, to relieve his feelings.

'Come on, get up! There's nothing the matter with you. Haven't broken your hip, have you? So why all this fuss? Talk about luck!'

The descent continued, even more slowly. The number of rests they took increased. When evening came, they had not yet reached the last zone of crevasses. They had to switch on their head-torches and look for faint traces of a track in the fading light.

'Perhaps we could get a bit of a move on!' muttered Maurice from time to time.

Léon Puidoux was disconcerted by all this forbearance. If he had been sworn at, he would have sought answering arguments, blamed the poor conditions, condemned the equipment, explained that their delay had made the climb longer and therefore more tiring, and so on and so forth, anything. Instead, he was brought face to face with himself, his utter weariness and the vague thoughts which failed to distract him but always homed in on a single goal – to get it over and done with.

It was nearly midnight when they arrived at the upper Plattje rocks where climbing parties unrope, still some way from the hut. Monsieur Puidoux was tottering with fatigue.

'I'm not going to walk another step!' he announced.

'We'd better spend the rest of the night here,' Maurice decided. 'You can't stand upright, and that's a fact. I've had enough myself. I brought some duvet jackets, even a little stove which I carried all the way up, for nothing yet. I'll heat us up some soup. We'll be better off finishing what's left of the descent by daylight.'

They huddled against a rock. The cold, though not intense, was unpleasant. Maurice tried to keep Monsieur Puidoux's morale up by telling him about other, far more uncomfortable bivouacs, and describing the excellent lunch they would have in Zermatt next day. Then, seeing that his client was shivering, he suggested moving on, now they had had a rest, and getting to the hut to spend the rest of the night in the warm, under good blankets. Monsieur Puidoux did not reply.

'We need to get our strength back, though!' Maurice persisted. 'The glaciers are beginning to open up. You saw that today. But the snow's melted, and it strikes me the Zmutt Ridge should be in good shape. Seeing we're on the spot, why don't we have a good night in Zermatt tomorrow and then go back up to the Hörnli Hut?'

But there was no response to indicate that Monsieur Puidoux had heard this last proposition.

In the small hours of the morning, the parties going up roused the two men who, when they were alone again, got ready to continue their descent. Despite his long climb yesterday and his uncomfortable night, Monsieur Puidoux seemed to have perked up considerably. After breakfast at the hut, he even set out on the return to Rotenboden with some vigour.

'He hasn't understood a thing!' thought Maurice. 'Good grief! How many trips like this will it take him?'

They settled down at last in the rack-railway and, searching for their pullovers in their rucksacks, instantly created around themselves with their crampons, ice-axes, cagoules and rope that muddle familiar to mountaineers, which the tourists sitting next to them contemplated with mingled disapproval and curiosity. Maurice was aware of the situation and told himself that even this must be hard to leave, the aftermath of battle when you feel different from other people, still being so near that star-bright world to which they have no access. But Léon Puidoux seemed far away from the scene. Huddled into a corner of his seat, he was gazing straight ahead, his eyes, their irises now paling, fixed on God knows what invisible point. All at once, an age-spotted hand pensively stroking his cheeks, where grey stubble was sprouting, he looked sadly at his guide and then, turning towards the window of the compartment where the Matterhorn was framed, outlined against the blue sky in the full glory of the morning, he whispered, very quietly, 'I'm through, Maurice.'

THE CURVED SPIRE

Stretched out on a warm granite slab, their boots, soaked with snow-melt, drying beside them, Philippe and François basked in the state of blissful torpor which follows a climb. They exchanged a few casual remarks from time to time as they idly scanned the huge Talèfre cirque which lay spread out before them.

'Hey!' Philippe exclaimed suddenly. 'Do you know what that curved rock spire is, to the left of the Aiguille de Talèfre? I don't know those parts too well.'

'What spire?' François wanted to know.

'There, on the ridge ... further over to the right!'

'Are you joking? The ridge is hundreds of metres long. There's the Aiguille de Savoie, I think, up there – more or less in the middle But I can't see what spire you're talking about.'

'Over to the right more! Look the way I'm pointing. Start at the bottom. There's a bergschrund forming an overhang ... are you with me?'

'Yes.'

'Well, go up diagonally along the rock face above, as far as that big patch of snow.'

'The one shaped like a shield?'

'That's right! After that there's a diagonal chimney which seems to link up with a thin icy couloir which must come up from below – but you can't make it out too well in this glare. Then you go up again and just to the right there's this odd curved spire. A beautiful summit! I'm surprised it isn't better known!'

'Hold on, I was following you at the start, but then you lost me. I can certainly see a whole series of little spikes and gendarmes on that ridge, but nothing that stands out particularly ... anyway, I'm sure I don't know their names!'

Philippe felt rather annoyed, and said no more. He thought he had made an interesting discovery in an area which few climbers visited and which it would be fun to explore. But François was feeling tired after their climb.

'I'm going to lie down for a bit in the hut,' he said. 'I didn't sleep a wink last night; it'll do me good. We're in no hurry, and we can go down when I've woken. Are you staying here?'

'Yes,' replied Philippe, who was amusing himself by looking for possible routes on the Curved Spire. He decided to mention it again when his friend had had his nap, but clouds rolled up over the ridges and soon there was nothing to be seen.

Philip forgot about the Curved Spire until, by chance, he returned to the Couvercle Hut a few days later with two other friends. From the terrace there, he saw his peak again, and he couldn't make out why this fine spire soaring to the sky, elegant as a bird's wing, was not better known. The narrow couloir which led up to it stood out clearly in the light of the setting sun.

'Do you know the name of that slanting spire, curving back a bit, up on the ridge opposite?' Philippe asked his friends. 'To the left of the Aiguille de Talèfre, but further away.'

'Where d'you mean, mate?'

'Over there, of course! Hang on, I'll show you exactly what I mean. It's superb . . .'

After some argument Philippe thought it best not to press the point.

'OK! I won't insist!' he conceded. 'Let's just say I've been seeing things!'

That evening he went out again, to inspect the Curved Spire by moonlight. He saw it yet again in the full blaze of the morning sun.

Back in the valley he thought about his peculiar experience and then went up to the Couvercle for the third time, this time by himself. And there was the Curved Spire.

He climbed it solo next morning, by the couloir. No problems, no mystery. A fine solid peak whose rocky summit formed a comfortable belvedere, giving superb views of the Talèfre glacier and the wild Italian side. The altimeter showed 3710 metres. Philip planned to visit the Maison de la Montagne as soon as he was down, to find out the real name of the Curved Spire and discover which route he had climbed.

The descent was a bit tricky because he had to climb down the couloir, which the sun had not yet reached, to get to the Talèfre cirque. It was his first solo climb, and when he was coming down towards the Mer de Glace a little later he felt well pleased with himself. But after such a splendid day, when he seemed to have had the mountain all to himself, it was irritating to be back among the crowds.

On the ladders which lead up from the glacier to the Montenvers Hotel, three young louts rushed down the rungs without taking the slightest notice of him, forcing him sideways so that he had to balance on the outside. And when he relieved his feelings by swearing at them, there was no response. Really, he thought, things are going from bad to worse on the mountains. You have a few magical hours and then return to mankind to find even your fellow mountaineers behaving like a bunch of oafs. All of them looking after Number One! Not so much as a 'Hello' or a 'Thank you'.

At the Montenvers it was worse. In the crowd of day-trippers Philippe had another mishap. It was definitely not his day any more. He just couldn't lay hands on his train ticket, which must have slipped through a hole in a pocket, and he didn't fancy walking the rest of the way down! He decided to buy another ticket and joined the queue behind a large man who was in charge of a group of noisy youngsters. The large man bought seven tickets, whereupon the ticket clerk abruptly shut the window, right in front of Philippe's nose, and disappeared into the depths of his office.

'Hurry along, please! The train's about to leave!' came the announcement.

Feeling very cross, Philippe tried to push his way in. And he succeeded: mingling with the gang of young people, he passed through the gate without any trouble and caught the train. His mixture of good and bad luck would have amused him if he hadn't been further irritated by the rough, off-hand behaviour of the passengers. Goodness knew he wasn't one to make a big thing about standards, but he did try not to jostle people or tread on their toes the way this bunch would have been treading on his the whole time if he hadn't kept avoiding them. All of this had pretty well wiped out the pleasure of his climb.

On arrival he elbowed his way out and jumped down on the platform with relief. An uneasy feeling came over him, however, when he was crossing the foot-bridge and met a middle-aged and very dignified couple who, straying slightly from their path, bumped right into him.

'Look where you're going, can't you?' growled Philippe. He got no reply.

But the awful truth dawned on him only a little further on, when he saw Catherine and Veronique leaving the C.A.F. and walking towards him.

'Hi there!' he called out. And he went towards them, beaming, arms outstretched.

They passed right through him, still carrying on with their conversation.

After this, Philippe had to acknowledge the facts. He alone had noticed the Curved Spire and he alone had climbed it. He alone now shared its nature. No one could see him, hear him or touch him any more; no one even knew that he was there, alive.

Francois was deeply affected by his friend's disappearance, and pinned an enlarged photo of him up over his desk. It had been taken on the terrace of the Couvercle Hut, on their return from their last climb together.

Next winter, whilst he was studying it sadly for the umpteenth time, an unexpected detail caught his attention.

'Hold on!' he muttered to himself. 'What's that more or less triangular summit up on the ridge, over to the left of the Aiguille de Talèfre? I never noticed it before. It's rather the shape of a sailing ship ... I say, that's rather a good name for it: l'Aiguille Brigantine! And it's bound to be an interesting climb. I must have a go at it next summer ...'

A CHANCE REUNION

William gave an impatient tug. He was obviously getting nowhere, trying to unravel this wretched cord. It was ridiculous that an ordinary bit of nylon fibre could act with such subtle and Machiavellian malevolence towards a rational being. In a twinkling it had tied itself into knots, with kinks, twists and tangles of every conceivable kind. Here you have a one-dimensional object in your hand which you'd think it would be simple enough to use, and it keeps on turning into a complicated construct in three dimensions, maybe even four . . . now then! Thread this bit here through that loop there . . . pull on this one . . . try slackening the central stopper . . . no, still not right . . .

William's bronzed face was burning slightly in the sunlight. He had forgotten the sun cream, so his nose would get red yet again . . . Okay, keep calm! Don't lose your temper, just have another go at undoing that knot.

All of a sudden the tangle gave way. Thank goodness for that! He handed the kite back to the little boy, telling him not to get the string into such a mess again, because Daddy had better things to do. He also reminded him not to go too far and be back in half an hour; Mummy would be expecting them for tea. The child shrieked with delight, grabbed the string and started running, giving a poor imitation of the sound of a jet plane taking off. William stretched out on his beach towel again with a sigh of satisfaction and, having scraped up some hot sand with his toes, enjoyed the delicious feeling of burying them in it. A good half-hour of peace lay ahead of him. You had to make the most of your holidays!

On hearing the sound of his voice, his neighbour on the left put down his detective story and half rose on his straw mat. He was a man of about forty with a bit of a paunch. A peculiar spotted cap protected the spreading bald patch on his scalp from the sun. Letting his sunglasses drop to the tip of his nose, he regarded William with a puzzled expression.

'William!' he murmured, eventually. 'William Martizay! Is it really you?'

The man thus addressed raised himself with a start of surprise.

'Good God!' he exclaimed. 'Cyprien! Heavens! What are you doing here?'

'What am I doing here? Well, can't you see? I'm at the seaside! It's you who ought to be asked that question. It's just part of my routine. Commuting, working, holidays, that's my life, and this is a good place for small children. Mind you, they're getting bigger now. I've got three. We spend nearly every day on the beach here at l'Estagnol. My in-laws have a cottage just inland, and they let us have it in August. How about you, though? I can't get over it! You, on the beach! Spending your holidays at the seaside! I'd never have thought of finding you anywhere else but in the mountains. Why, I even had an idea that you'd turned professional. I mean, after coming out top in the guides' course . . . one of the most talented climbers of your generation, and when I say talented, I mean talented! Fanatical about it too! I'm not in touch with that crowd any more, but if I'd been told you were teaching at the École Nationale de Ski et d'Alpinisme these days I'd have believed it! Instead of which I find you here at the height of the holiday season, lying on a beach where the landscape is decidely flat apart from certain feminine curves! Last time I saw you, you were about to leave for Kenchojemal.'

'Well, that certainly goes back a long way! I did go, yes. A terrific expedition. We all made it to the summit.'

'And then?'

William heaved a sigh. His friend's remarks had brought the whole of his past before his mind's eye. Feeling a kind of need to explain himself, he started his tale.

'It's all rather stupid, really,' he said. 'You know, climbing's OK when you're young. As you get older you sober up; you realise there are other things in life. You settle down, change, adapt to circumstances . . .'

'Sure, that's true for most of us. I gave it all up a long time ago. But you were so bitten! I still can't understand . . . I'd have sworn nothing would ever have dragged you away from the mountains! Was it an accident, or some other kind of a problem?'

'Nothing like that, I tell you. It just worked out that way. Quite straightforward. There's really nothing to tell. I had a few girl-friends, like everybody else, but it's a fact that only the mountains really counted . . . in fact, I was rather wary of women. Too many of them hang around climbing circles to catch someone they consider a sort of hero – they don't care about anything else, they haven't a clue what climbing's really about. But Martine was different . . .'

Cyprien suppressed a smile.

'Here was a girl who really tried to understand what the game was about. When she happened along with some friends, it was pure chance.

But she had guts and immediately got into the run of things. I didn't fall for her straight away – she was just around the place. She asked my advice, wanted me to explain things. She soon got to know the names of the Aiguilles and even of the routes on them. She encouraged us, took an interest in our plans, started buying her own gear. She looked quite well in her breeches and her helmet. As a beginner, she went on climbs with groups organised by the French Alpine Club or the Guides' Bureau. Sometimes she was happy just to come up to the hut with us; she was always cheerful, and she cooked splendid little meals concocted out of next to nothing – pepper steaks, flambéed omelettes, she really had the knack of it. She wasn't trying to catch you or anything like that – she simply wanted to be part of the scene.'

'And so you married her and here you are at the seaside!'

'No, not at all! Certainly not! I told you, this girl was really understanding. You could feel relaxed with her, go for a walk without feeling that she was only waiting for the chance to fall into your arms. Back in Paris, she joined our group walking or climbing at Fontainebleau. Come rain, snow or wind, she was always there, never complaining, never being difficult. At Easter we all organised a weekend at Chamonix and did the Vallée Blanche. It was very warm and towards the end – you know, below Montenvers where you traverse those gullies which descend into the forest – she was caught by a small avalanche which swept her down the slope. We were terrified! We rushed down after her and found her, hardly buried at all, nothing wrong with her except for a badly sprained ankle. She insisted on carrying on down to the bottom with us, even though the pain did cause the occasional moan and a few tears. I kept my eye on her, stayed close to her, and I must say I admired her!'

'So she came out of it all right?'

'Yes, of course! But she could have killed herself – I mean, suppose her head had struck a rock? They took her to hospital and kept her in for twenty-four hours, for observation. I went to see her. I even gave up a skiing trip to Mont Blanc – with a helicopter – we were going to do next day. She thought so little about herself that she reproached me for having done so. It must have been about then I really fell in love with her. She wasn't like other girls. Definitely not the sort to cause difficulties. And I was afraid her accident might have put her off mountains, make her turn to other interests. She did sometimes seem a little remote, and I wondered what she was thinking about – or who she was thinking about. I felt that she wasn't really paying attention to me; she seemed preoccupied with other things. And I told myself that here was my ideal woman and I might lose her. Does that make you laugh?'

'No, it doesn't make me laugh at all. It's a very nice story. But it still doesn't explain why I find you here on the beach at l'Estagnol.'

'It's simple, I told you, but the story is of no great interest.'

'Oh yes, it is! I'm intrigued. What happened next?'

'Well, nothing in particular. We drew closer to each other, went out together, became practically engaged. The next summer we went climbing, just the two of us. She was less fit, unfortunately, her ankle kept bothering her . . .'

Cyprien could visualise the set-up perfectly. His friend's story brought the whole mountaineering scene he used to know so well before his mind's eye. He even felt he could finish the tale more accurately than his interlocutor. Without doubt, the girl Martine had been quite sincere. She had simply followed her female instinct. The urgings of love, the prospect of nest-building, would soon have overcome her interest in hut walks, the early departures, the cold, the heavy rucksack, the exhaustion and the crumbling moraines . . . Cyprien could just see her worrying over the injured ankle which saved her from too-long walks. He could sense her relief when a bad weather forecast held out the hope of a romantic episode outside the mountain valley. As for William, he was under her spell by now and blind to all these shortcomings. Why does every human being think himself unique when faced with a situation which millions of others have known before? And why is it love, in particular, which convinces those under its influence that nothing like it has ever happened before, now or since? William used to be on his guard against women, regarding them as a threat to his special relationship with the mountains. But when the day came he had succumbed like everyone else, and only chance could now determine the attitude of his chosen one towards her rival of granite and ice.

William brushed some sand from his arm and stretched out on his towel with a grunt of pleasure.

'What a beautiful day!' he muttered. 'There's a sea breeze, so the sun isn't too hot. Eh, what was I saying?'

'You were telling me about your first alpine season together.'

'Oh, yes. Well, I've told you the gist of it . . . how we got to know each other and all that. I'll only bore you if I go on.'

'Not at all, I assure you! So you got married?'

'Yes, we got married the following winter. Thank goodness, I'd found that *rara avis* – a woman who understood everything and could accept my climbing, even if she did much less of it herself. To be frank, I didn't much care for your sarcastic tone just now. Martine isn't the scheming sort who'd think of nothing but how to get me to the seaside. We went on holidaying in the mountains for several years. Of course there were some little changes, a few mutual adjustments . . . that's marriage, after all. For instance, she wasn't so keen on Hubert, my regular climbing partner . . . she showed me he wasn't as straight-forward as I used to think. You have to make certain concessions, and you find plenty of compensations for them. We were quite a little clique, me and Martine and her friends. Whenever they came to our house, there was a place at our table for them, and Martine's a good cook when she puts her mind to it. You can just imagine how popular she was – letting her husband go climbing and welcoming his friends. You could say I'd succeeded where many others have failed!'

'And you went on doing good climbs? Expeditions?'

'Well, let's not exaggerate . . . after all, bachelors go on expeditions. It means so long away from home, endless preliminaries . . . But good climbs, sure! With rather more caution, naturally. Martine's first pregnancy made her feel nervous, but she still let me go climbing, and I was the one who set limits on myself. You can guess what happened next . . . well, a man can't take the same risks when he's got a child. Or something silly happens to get in the way. I was going to do the Frêney Pillar once, it was in good condition and all that, but I'd forgotten the baby was to be vaccinated in two days' time and I'd promised to be there. Okay, so I went back to my partner, we changed the plan and did a one-day climb on the Peigne . . . quite hard all the same, mind you! Martine never complained . . . it's just that I occasionally got carried away by my old habits, and then she would very quietly remind me of our commitments. And then, when our daughter was born, I realised I'd better wind down, but that didn't prevent us from spending another two or three summers in the mountains. But not for climbing, of course. And after that, well, if you can't climb why not have a bit of a change? The weather suits everyone here in the south . . . so there we are! I've given up climbing, yes, but it's not the way you thought. I gave up of my own free will, you might say, and Martine didn't come into it at all.'

Cyprien regarded his friend affectionately. He remembered that only a few moments ago he had barely recognised the young tiger of the old days days in this middle-aged gentleman with his spreading paunch and greying temples. Who knew whether things hadn't turned out for the best after all? If William had followed his calling he might even now be lying at the bottom of a crevasse, frozen stiff, instead of sunning himself on the beach at l'Estagnol. That's life!

'We must meet again!' he said warmly. 'Are you staying here long?'

'Another fortnight . . . excuse me, I have to find my little boy. Martine's expecting him back for tea. Where on earth has he got to?'

The two men scrutinised the motley crowd of parents and children thronging the beach or paddling in the water, to no avail.

Suddenly, Cyprien said, 'That's not him, is it, up on those rocks right at the end of the beach?'

'Oh, my God, so it is!' exclaimed William. 'We'll be late home, and I'll be in trouble! That child's a real little devil! Always thinking up something new . . . always climbing something, anything he comes across!'

A TOUR OF THE MASSIF

'Ladies and gentlemen . . . today, Day 127 of Year 256 of the Third Galaxiad, you are seated on board Bubble Z 71849, which is taking you to see some astonishing relics of ancient civilizations. You have communicated your genetic imprints to the device, and each of you is now receiving our commentary in his or her national language. Welcome to our foreign friends! We congratulate you on choosing not to employ the facilities of modern technology for this leap into the past. You have not, accordingly, been dematerialized. You have not had yourselves transmitted in the usual form of radio-electric signals. You are here in the flesh. And having chosen to arrive by ancient means of transport, whose quaint charm you will have appreciated, you have taken, respectively, fifty-eight seconds to come from Paris, one minute three seconds from Pforzheim, one minute forty seconds from London, three minutes forty-five seconds from Abu Dhabi, and a whole eight minutes twenty-seven seconds to get here from Melbourne . . . We would like to apologize for the sixty-two hours you have had to spend going through customs, police, judicial, medical and psychiatric procedures, fiscal and parafiscal formalities, baggage checks, thought checks, and all the other examinations which, as you know, are the small but inevitable price to be paid for progress. So here we all are, and we hope you will enjoy your journey to a world of which even the memory has been lost.

Our tour will proceed along the following lines. Before you, you see a gaseous screen held in place by magnetism. When I say "On your left" or "On your right", those passengers sitting on the side in question will, if they wish, be able to see the natural phenomenon, curiosity or site I mention as it actually is, while the others will see it appear on the screen. Passengers wishing to spare themselves the trouble of turning their heads will be able to view the entire spectacle on the screen alone, but in order to make the most of your visit we do advise you to look straight through the side of the bubble from time to time.

The tour will be conducted in three stages, and the remarkable sights you are about to see relate to one of the few areas of high-lying land to have been conserved on this planet as archaeological monuments. It is known as the Mont Blanc massif. Let me just remind you that the other such highland regions still intact are Ayers Rock, Australia; Geiranger Fjord, Norway; and Mount Washington, USA. The size, extent and altitude of the Mont Blanc massif makes it the largest of these conservation areas.

You will remember that before the continents of this planet were flattened to a uniform altitude of 8 metres above sea level for obvious reasons of logical utility, the whole surface of the earth presented irregularities such as those you are about to see, more particularly during the third part of our tour. We would therefore advise persons of a sensitive nature to close their eyes when the pictures we show appear excessively alarming.

There now follows a brief historical note on the levelling of the planet. The first attempts date back to the twentieth century (old reckoning). They were made in Singapore, where, with a dynamism which was surprisingly in advance of its time, engineers conceived the idea of flattening hills so as to convey the material thus obtained into the sea, thereby increasing the surface area of the island. This example was soon being followed all over the world. India and the adjacent countries, which had severe over-population problems, set about constructing the great Himalayan Peninsula, using the mountain range of the same name. The entire operation was completed on an international scale several centuries ago, and we should respectfully salute the work and the perseverance of our ancestors, who have spared us the problems, the interrupted vision, and all the anxieties once caused by irregularities in the earth's surface.

It is very difficult to know and understand past civilizations. Not so long ago they still retained all their mystery. But thanks to patient research based on the study of archaeological documents together with historical sources and scientific analysis, our scholars have reached some remarkable conclusions casting light on the customs and cultures of the past.

You see before you a concrete wall three hundred metres high, towards the top of which we are rising to reach the entry hatch. We shall be passing through it any moment now ... There we go! We are now entering a vast concrete parallelepiped in a delightfully archaic style. Observe the four high walls which form its sides. This rectangular pit is known as the *Servoz Lock*. Linguists have succeeded in ascertaining the etymology of this name, a corruption of the pious prayer to the ancient goddess of fortune, "Save us, Luck!", which people were in the habit of uttering as they entered this narrow corridor.

The *Servoz Lock* is the museum proper, and the first stage of our tour will be conducted here. Treasures of great rarity, a precious testimony to life in primitive times, are assembled all along the walls.

On your right, first, you will see in this vast display case two immense conical cylinders with various appendages. These are very curious specimens of a once living species known as *trees*. Such vegetable beings grew rapidly and reached amazing heights. Their ramifications, the remains of which you can see, were covered with either short filaments known as *needles* or small pieces of vegetation called *leaves*. The two giant specimens you see here belong to the species called *Spruce*, employed by our ancestors for humanitarian purposes. It appears that thanks to the use of this species, human beings succeeded in shielding their neighbours from the terrifying sight of the mountains and even from exposure to daylight, which they obviously feared.

In the next display case you will see some smaller cylinders exhibited. These are also *trees* of different kinds, known respectively, from left to right, as *Hornbeam*, *Beech*, *Birch* and *Larch*. Their needles or leaves changed colour depending on the season of the year, disappearing entirely at certain times. Hardened to all the ferocity of nature, our ancestors seem to have survived such incidents without feeling too much stress, although we would now find them terrifying.

In the case on the left, notice an exceptional live exhibit of an enormous animal species now on its way to extinction: the *Cow*, whose head bears curious, slightly curved, rigid antennae. Today there are only about a dozen representatives of the species left in the world. The *Cow* you see here is a female. Biologists are trying to save the species by endeavouring to get it to reproduce, and to that end the curator of the *Servoz Lock* Museum recently managed to borrow a male of the same species from the zoo of His Majesty Tsar Nicholas XXXIV, Emperor of All the Russias. But unfortunately it proved impossible to mate them. It seems that these animals can no longer reproduce in captivity.

Next, on your right, in a crystalline case, you will see a remarkable glazed cabin dangling from several metal strands. This was one of the methods employed by people in olden times to surmount the problem of the different levels found on the surface of the earth. They had yet stranger devices, and even used to move about with the aid of their own anterior and posterior limbs, thereby maintaining a somewhat precarious equilibrium.

In the case on the left, notice several curios of a rather special nature. You must know that, ludicrous as it may seem today, our ancestors fed through their mouths. This case, therefore, contains a collection of several shards and remains of utensils such as they used for preparing or keeping food. Note the remarkable aluminium *Saucepan*, almost intact, dating from the middle of the twentieth century (old reckoning), the amazing fragment of a *Bottle* in delicately tinted translucent glass, and the so-called set of *Cutlery* in a white plastic material of astonishing delicacy. Beside these exhibits you will see the commercial sign of a public place called a *Restaurant*, where it was possible for people to eat in company. Specialists in calligraphy have deciphered the names of several dishes identified by archaeologists as regional specialities of the former Chamonix valley. They read, from top to bottom: *Pizza, Paella, Couscous, Hamburger*.

Finally, on your right, you will see some venerable relics. These are the bones of several local benefactors described as *Property Developers, Building Contractors, Structural Engineers*, and sometimes *Mayors*. Although the precise significance of these titles is lost in the mists of time, humanity has retained a deep respect for those who bore them. Very likely they were High Priests who contributed to the erection of the first temples of progress.

We are coming to the end of this stage of our tour, and we now enter another passage passing through the wall which closes the southern extremity of the *Servoz Lock*, leading to the *Sublime Concrete Trench*, known in primitive times as the *Chamonix Valley*.

Linguists have not yet determined the exact etymology of this very ancient term. Referring to certain pages in Du Cange's *Dictionary*, a work dating from the *Age of Writing*, some believe that the word *Chamonix* derives from the Low Latin *Chamonagium*, meaning *uncultivated land*: a plausible derivation, since this seems to have been one of the first places where humanity definitively triumphed over nature. According to others, the term may come from another Latin expression, *Campus munitus*: the word *Campus*, meaning in American neo-Latin 'University', would seem to indicate that the former Chamonix Valley was one of the cultural shrines of antiquity, while the adjective *munitus*, 'closed', specified that it was reserved for an intellectual élite of a particularly elevated standard.

Be that as it may, you will be able to admire one of the first technical achievements of the concrete industry of the beginning of the third millennium, an ancient masterpiece whose boldness is surprising when you think of the rudimentary methods with which it was executed.

Here we are. The *Sublime Concrete Trench* once had irregular, unstable slopes, partially planted with *spruce trees* or strewn with formless rocks – a spectacle of confusion and horror, more particularly because the many precipitations occurring here as snow set off disordered falls known as *avalanches*. To correct all these unpleasant features, a brilliant architect had the idea of covering the area entirely with concrete tiers to a height of a thousand metres. Admire the skill of the work! The harmonious succession of the tiers themselves! The perfect alternation of walls and terraces which, while entirely concealing the former shape of the terrain, are drained by a cleverly designed system of channels which direct the meltwater to the *Channel of the Arve* which you see at the bottom of the Trench, a last vestige of those running waters which used to meander over the surface of the earth! The secret of making concrete is now lost, and modern science is unable to reproduce that strange material which allied strength to the most incredible lightness! See the fine grain, the delicate texture! Admire, also, the quaint charm of the so-called *Blockhouse* architectural style, old-fashioned, to be sure, but aesthetically so pure! This is a major work of the pre-ontistic period!

Dwellings let into the walls allowed the *Sublime Concrete Trench* to accommodate up to eight hundred and fifty thousand people during the pilgrimage seasons. The site is now deserted and classified as an historical monument.

Certain ancient inscriptions may be deciphered above the doors of some of these cave dwellings. One, which you will see on your left, reads *E.N.S.A.*, probably an abbreviation standing for the Elevated New Salvation Army. A little further on, see the *Hypermarket*, whose many handsomely proportioned aisles served as an ambulatory for philosophers. Finally, notice the great cavern of the *Club Méditerranée*, whose name links it to the ancient civilizations of Greece: this was an academy of poet-philosophers who endeavoured, by practising rigorous asceticism, to revive the stern customs of Sparta.

The terraces of the *Sublime Concrete Trench* extend along a length of some twenty kilometres. We are now coming to the eastern end, where you can see the superb *Balme Amphitheatre*, the terminating point of the entire edifice.

On the third stage of our tour we shall be viewing mountainous country in its natural state, and it is at this point that we advise persons of an impressionable nature to look away. We are now gaining altitude, rising above the top terrace, and we can see the high peaks of our planet conserved in their primitive state. It was amidst such visions of terror, such nightmare landscapes, that our ancestors had to survive. Observe the anarchy of this wild, three-dimensional and irregular scenery!

Long years of archaeological digs have made it possible to excavate and classify these peaks. Finally, scholars have recently discovered why hundreds of thousands of people used to visit these high places every year. The phenomenon was connected with a cult. Primitive societies, fervently religious in tone, used to subordinate all their activities to liturgical practices linked to their beliefs. The Mont Blanc massif, among other sites, was a place of pilgrimage for devotees of the particularly fanatical sect of *Mountaineers*, which did not shrink from human sacrifice.

Worshippers came here from all over the world, and a tunnel was even driven through the base of the mountain to make it easier for them to come and go. Some of the faithful were content with mere contemplation, but true initiates went in for very much stranger practices: a number of them, for instance, gave themselves up to acts of penitence and purification, setting out from holy places called *Huts*. We are about to see one such shrine, which has come down to us in an excellent state of preservation. We are now entering a hanging valley where we shall see the *Argentière Hut*, an edifice of great antiquity. From this place processions of penitents, ready for the ultimate sacrifice and tied together in two or threes by nylon ropes, used to set out in stages throughout the night, carrying small sacred lanterns and sometimes escorted by priestly instructors called *Guides*.

The *Argentière Hut* is built in the purest neo-futuristic Savoyard style. It proves that our ancestors themselves could hardly endure the sight of the terrible mountains, for the architect cleverly designed the windows of the common room to show only the foot of the slopes, a very wise precaution! According to a recent theory which I will allow myself to mention here, the *Argentière Hut* was reserved for major penitents with a very great deal on their consciences, as witness a peculiar detail of its design whereby the dormitories were situated not above but below the common room, so that the uninterrupted succession of nocturnal departures made it impossible to rest at all in the rooms intended for that purpose: an unparalleled refinement of cruelty, if this theory is correct!

Inside the small reliquary built beside the hut you will see a display of several votive offerings which the pilgrims deposited at various points of their climb, consecrating the alliance between mankind and the mountain. Excavated not long ago from the glacial strata which had preserved them until our time, these offerings have recently been identified by scholars. Detailed laboratory work will now undoubtedly determine their respective socio-religious functions. Here are several magnificent examples of the containers known as *Cans*: carefully tin-plated metallic cylinders of admirably regular shape. See also a very pretty specimen of a supple *Plastic Bag* in two colours . . . a fragment of a *Cigarette*, ritually charred at one end . . . an interesting fossilized *Cheese Rind* . . . a small cardboard container, parallelepiped in shape, bearing an inscription which unfortunately is partly erased but seems to read *Sanitary Tamp* . . . a curious *Electric Battery* bearing the cabbalistic signs + and − . Finally, the most amazing and certainly the most beautiful of the discoveries: this extraordinary *Orange Peel*, removed in a single spiral whorl! One hardly knows which to admire more: the prodigious artistic sense or the skilful mastery of technique which went into the creation of this masterpiece.

We are now mounting above the *Sublime Concrete Trench* to visit the two principal sanctuaries. On your left, pointing towards the sky, on the peak called the *Aiguille du Midi*, observe the superb rocket-shaped monument to the god *Herz*. The god *Herz* was the most powerful deity of ancient mythology, and was married to the goddess *Teevee*. The worshippers of the sacred couple were numerous in all countries of the world – the *Mountaineering* sect was only one branch – and devotees spent several hours a day in prayer before a domestic altar called *The Telly*. As a sign of gratitude and veneration, they placed a curious item of metallic tracery known as an *Aerial* on the roofs of their houses. They believed that this device established some kind of direct relationship between themselves and the divine couple.

Every year, in the two main pilgrimage seasons of summer and winter, the faithful would come in hundreds of thousands to worship at the monument to the god *Herz*. Some, wishing to get closer, had themselves raised to a level with it by means of the small glazed cabin we admired in the *Servoz Lock*. During the winter pilgrimage season there was even a custom whereby the most fanatical, instead of returning by the same means of transport, flung themselves down the vertiginous snow slopes you see below our bubble. When they did this they tied long spatulas known as *Skis* to their feet. The *Skis* had been devised especially for this purpose, and thanks to the force of gravity helped them to fling themselves into the abyss. Imagine the zeal and exaltation of the devotees of these sects who gave themselves up to ritual acts of so terrifying a nature!

Around the monument to the god *Herz*, in several display cases, you will see various cult objects used by the *Mountaineering* sect exhibited. First, here are the two spatulas or *Skis* I mentioned just now. Here is the great ceremonial pectoral called the *Altimeter*, worn ritually around the neck; its design, which is very delicate and precise, is protected by an extremely thin circle of glass. Here are shoes with soles bearing spikes called *Crampons*, as used by certain fakirs. To your left, a very fine example of a sacred lantern, the *Head Torch*, made of aluminium, glass and plastic, fitted together with the utmost precision. A purple *Rope*, which linked the penitents together, and a Goretex *Cagoule*, worn in processions. A thick *Duvet* jacket, whose purpose has not yet been ascertained for sure: according to some archaeologists, it was meant to impress enemies, in which case we may suppose that sacred conflicts took place between rival sects. This hypothesis is confirmed by the recent discovery of the *Ice Axe*, a kind of asymmetrical hatchet which must have been a formidable weapon. Finally, since we are speaking of the civilization of the *Age of Writing* in its heyday, you will see, underneath this reinforced dome, the three holy books: the *Guide Michelin*, the *Guide Bleu* and the *Guide Vallot*. The texts have not yet been decoded by specialists.

Our tour is now coming to an end. You have only to admire the final curiosity, on the north side of the Trench and facing the monument to the god *Herz*: a sanctuary where the faithful indulged in their various liturgical practices. This is the *Great Altar of the Brévent*. Sacred libations were poured in the small temple known as the *Bar*, which you now see on your left.

After this journey through time, which has taken us back to the very roots of humanity's artistic and cultural heritage, a journey brought to life by the intuition and erudition of our learned archaeologists, we now return to the *Servoz Lock*. We feel sure you will never forget the moving message from history which has just been transmitted to you over the millennia. The tour is now over. Please do not forget a tip for the guide.'

MY UNKNOWN FRIEND

To Peter Drummond Smith and Georges Bettembourg,
my almost unknown friends

People talk about premonitions; it seems odd that there isn't a word for the opposite phenomenon. Isn't it even more common for precisely the opposite of what we expected to occur? Sometimes you feel anxious, as if aware of some veiled menace and ready for disaster to strike. But nothing happens, and day follows day in a calm and regular manner. Time passes, anxieties fade, and you forget that your premonitions never materialized. While at other times, when you thought you could bask in tranquil contentment, free from care, something will suddenly happen to disrupt your whole life, so unexpectedly that you can hardly take it in.

That's what happened to me one July evening I shall never forget. However, there seemed nothing in prospect but pleasant relaxation that fine afternoon. I was just back from climbing the North Face of the Dent d'Hérens, an ambition twice thwarted by bad weather in previous seasons, so that my friend Serge and I had set off with superstitious glances at the cloudless sky, hardly daring to believe it was going to smile on us at last. And now our hard-won triumph seemed all the sweeter because we had wanted it so long. We had bivouacked on the way down, setting out again early in the morning on the long traverse which took us over the Col de Valpelline in the direction of Switzerland. Serge, my usual climbing companion, then had to leave at once for Grenoble after only a short four-day break. I was on holiday, although I had brought some work and an article to finish, so as I waited for his return in the near future I planned to enjoy the wonderful rest you get only at the price of prolonged physical effort, particularly a long climb in the mountains.

I had made myself comfortable on the small lawn in front of the flatlet I'd bought the previous year. I had showered and shaved, and I had ingredients in the kitchen for a good dinner, which I planned to wash down with a bottle of Auvernier, a present from friends in Neuchâtel. All I regretted was the absence of Serge: recalling our climb in detail – even better, sharing our silences – would have helped us to re-live the two days we had just spent together in the wild all over again. But here I was on my own, surrounded by all the stuff I'd put out to dry: ropes, boots, sleeping bags, climbing jackets, all the motley, vivid clutter of the aftermath of a climb. I had poured myself a cold beer and was looking at the Chamonix Aiguilles and the light, pale clouds floating lazily around them. Automatically, my eyes followed the routes I had already taken; I noted the conditions, the snow still picking out the Reynier and Fontaine ledge system on the Blaitière, and the grey ice beginning to appear on the upper part of the Frendo Spur. But what chiefly occupied my mind was the previous day's climb, which seemed both infinitely near and very far away. I was exhausted. I could feel the pain the weight of my sack had left in my shoulders. It was all past history now, yet when I closed my eyes, I saw behind their lids visions of steep and never-ending rocks intermingled with ice, my last remaining clear impressions of the face we had climbed.

The contrast between our climb itself and my present serenity gave me a wonderful sense of fulfilment. And just as I was savouring it, the door-bell rang. I sighed heavily and then called, 'Come in!' since that's expected of you, but I was determined to get rid of my unwanted visitor quickly.

The door opened, revealing two familiar faces which I would happily have welcomed at any other time. They belonged to Robert and Étienne, young men of about twenty and very good climbers. They joined me in the garden, looking anxious.

'Do you speak English, Patrick?' asked Robert, as we shook hands.

'Yes, very well,' I told him. 'I have an Irish grandmother; I'm practically bilingual. You want me to translate something for you?'

'No,' said Étienne. 'Well, we don't know exactly what we do want … that's the trouble. We're afraid an Englishman camping near us may have had an accident, but we aren't sure.'

I could see complications which didn't appeal to me at all looming on the horizon. The evening was too fine for such things, too calm, too peaceful, and I was too tired. I was not interested in the case of the unknown Englishman. There are plenty of mountaineering accidents which *are* your own business: no need to go adding those which aren't. In fact I'd have preferred to steer clear of the whole affair. I couldn't shake off the contentment which had such total command of me a moment ago, just like that.

'Have a beer?' I asked the lads. It was a way of drawing them into my own world. But once I'd given them their beers they went back to theirs.

'This is what's bothering us,' said Robert. 'This guy was camping near us. He spoke good French, and we got on well. He lent us his camping stove once when we ran out of gas. The friend he was expecting hadn't been able to come, so we gathered he was going to join some other friends in Zermatt. In fact we didn't expect to see him again because we were off to do the Rochefort/Jorasses traverse, and we left on Friday. That was the 11th. We slept at the Torino Hut that night, and have only just got back down. His tent was still there with something pinned to it: a note which was already there when we started out. We looked at it. It's dated the 11th, and this is the 14th. Étienne has an idea he saw this guy leave with his mountaineering gear, but he wasn't taking a lot of notice, and he can't remember if it was the morning of the 10th or the 11th anyway.'

'More likely the 10th,' suggested Étienne. But I can't swear to it.'

'It may not be anything serious,' Robert went on. 'And it's probably silly to worry when nobody's asked you to do anything . . . but on the other hand, suppose he's in trouble somewhere? We thought you could look round his tent with us, see if there are any clues, talk to other English climbers . . . '

I realized, chiefly, that Étienne and Robert weren't appealing to my linguistic skills so much as to my extra ten years of experience. Unsure whether they were sticking their oar in where it wasn't wanted, they were after an opinion which would let them off shouldering the responsibility entirely on their own. It still seemed none of my business.

'I think you're getting alarmed rather too soon,' I said. 'There's nothing to say that there's been an accident, or the man's on his own. He may have met friends and gone on a long route. Or a series of climbs. It's wonderful weather.'

'Yes, but he had a date in Zermatt,' Robert repeated. 'And if he'd gone there he'd have taken his tent.'

'Oh, all right, let's go,' I sighed.

Robert and Étienne were camping near Le Biollay, in a pretty little wood. They led me to a small blue tent with a note pinned near the opening. It was indeed dated July 11th and signed by one Andy, who said he was leaving for the Dolomites, which didn't get us much further. I opened the zip fastener. Inside the tent, neatly arranged, were an inflatable mattress, a rolled sleeping bag, several garments and pieces of mountaineering equipment, but no rucksack, ice axe, crampons or helmet, which obviously suggested that the occupant of the tent was out climbing. A mess tin held several mouldy peaches. I went out to throw them away, using this as an excuse to join Étienne and Robert in questioning neighbouring campers. They hadn't noticed anything, hadn't seen anything, and anyway most of them had arrived only that long weekend. I went back into the tent to put the mess tin back, and suddenly jumped in surprise. On top of a carton full of books and papers lay the latest issue of *Arabian Studies*, in which I had just published an article on the first Imams of Nizwa.

'What does your bloke do for a living?' I asked, putting my head out.

Two shakes of the head answered me. I opened the journal, which had little pencil annotations here and there. Two of them were about my article. One picked up an error of transliteration which I had unfortunately failed to notice in the proofs, the other made a very interesting suggestion about possible continuity with the Julanda régime.

'What was his name?' I asked again.

'Peter . . . I think,' hazarded Étienne.

I hesitated to pursue my enquiries further, but I was beginning to feel interested in the Englishman, and since I was here I ought at least to try getting some clear idea. I soon found the name I was after on the flyleaf of a book and some envelopes addressed *Poste restante* to Chamonix: a name not unknown to me, since it was that of Peter Westmorland, the author of a fascinating study putting forward new hypotheses about the presumed site of the ancient city of Omana. I'd expected to be in touch with him some time or other, and here he was sharing my other passion, my love of climbing!

'Well, what do you think?' asked Robert.

His question brought me back to the problem of the Englishman's disappearance. Now that the person concerned was taking shape in my mind as a very intelligent man, I felt there ought to be some perfectly logical explanation. I glanced through several more papers, frowning as I found a letter with a Bristol letterhead which did indeed make a date with its recipient to meet in Zermatt on July 13th. I reassured myself by thinking that a letter meant nothing: there was such a thing as the telephone, and appointments could be changed, postponed or cancelled. And yet I was beginning to share my young friends' anxiety. Further searching turned up an address: the address of Lady Westmorland, Kermist Hall, Widecombe, Devon, on the back of two envelopes I did not venture to open. However, I memorized it.

'What do we do now?' asked Étienne.

I felt myself suffering the same uncertainty the two lads had been feeling when they called on me. Raising the alarm seemed unjustified in the absence of more information, especially when it was for someone we hardly knew, someone who had left us no instructions and who might have perfectly good reasons to go off. And if he were up in the mountains, we had no way of knowing which route he had taken or what sector ought to be searched. But suppose Peter Westmorland really was in difficulties somewhere? Had we a right to do nothing? Oughtn't we to warn his family – consult them?

'Let's wait until tomorrow morning,' I decided. 'If he isn't back by then, come and tell me. Then we may have to take action.'

I went home feeling rather anxious, still weighing up the pros and cons of the whole business in my mind. I couldn't recover either my delightful sense of tranquillity or the pleasure I'd been anticipating that evening. The Aiguilles, after burning with rosy light in the last rays of the sun, had melted into a chilly grey. I ate my dinner quickly and then, unable to wait any longer, reached for the telephone and asked International Directory Enquiries for the phone number of the Westmorlands of Widecombe, Devon. I got it a few moments later, and without stopping to think, I began dialling the United Kingdom code. Then I hung up again. Whatever had happened, nothing could be done that evening, and it was better to let the family pass a quiet night. However, thinking more clearly now, I called the police mountain rescue service to find out if any Englishmen, and in particular a man called Peter Westmorland, had recently been involved in accidents in the massif. The reply was reassuring. Apart from three Spaniards who had fallen on the Aiguille du Chardonnet, the only accidents over the past few days had been minor ones, and none of them involved English climbers.

Then I went to bed, hoping for good news in the morning, and the racket of the July 14th firework displays scarcely disturbed my sleep at all. I was still asleep when the phone rang. It was broad daylight, and Robert was calling to say there was no news yet.

I breakfasted thoughtfully, and decided I really would consult the family now. Dialling the number and hearing the short, sharp ringing of a British phone, I imagined a green valley in Dartmoor, a many-gabled English house, a lawn of fine turf, flower-beds and old trees, and I felt guilty about importing what might be unfounded anxiety into those peaceful surroundings. I decided to be as reassuring as possible. Anyway, who knew whether our absent friend might not have had to pay a brief visit home? Perhaps I was about to speak to him in person and tell him about our suspicions and anxieties.

A very clear female voice replied, bringing me down to earth with a jolt. Feeling ready to curse myself for embarking on this, I asked awkwardly if I was speaking to Lady Westmorland, related to Peter Westmorland, on holiday in Chamonix.

'Lady Westmorland's my mother,' said the voice. 'I'm Peter's sister Dorothy. I hope nothing's happened to him?'

'No, no, certainly not!' I replied. 'It's nothing serious. I kind of phoned on impulse; I'm sure it's ridiculous. I'm resting after a climb. But two friends of mine who were camping near your brother were surprised not to see him ... not to see him for rather a long time, that's all. We opened up his tent, I found your address, and I just thought it would be best to call you, find out if by any chance you have any recent news.'

'I must shut the door,' said the girl. 'Wait a moment.'

She soon resumed our interrupted conversation.

'I'd better tell you something,' she said in a low voice. 'My father, who was very old, died last winter, and my parents had already lost their elder son in a stupid accident when he was ten. My mother isn't strong. Peter and I try to spare her worry. That's why I went to close the door before talking frankly to you. Now, tell me how long ago Peter disappeared.'

Briefly, I told her the circumstances so far as I knew them, trying to sound optimistic and saying how often, in the mountains, you're apt to start worrying for no reasons, which was probably the case this time. Finally, I stressed the fact that it was beautiful weather in Chamonix and all over the Alps, and passed on the reassuring reply elicited by my call to the mountain rescue service.

'All the same ... ' said the girl the other end. 'I know Peter was definitely expecting to join his friends in Zermatt. He mentioned it in his last letter. And I do think I ought to let my mother know about this. She wouldn't understand if I didn't, after a phone call like this. Is there any way you could get more information at your end?'

'Of course! I'll do everything I can.'

'Give me your phone number. I'll call you back anyway.'

A few moments later the mountain rescue police confirmed that there had been no report of any accident to a group of English climbers or a solitary Englishman since the previous evening. I also called the four or five principal guarded huts in the massif to find out if a climber called Peter Westmorland had been there during the last few days. My enquiries met with a pleasant response, but got me nowhere.

Late that afternoon Dorothy Westmorland called back. I thought her voice sounded strained.

'My mother's decided we ought to come over,' she said. 'If it's only to find Peter safe and sound, all the better. If anything else ... well, if anything else has happened, it's better not to lose any time. We'd rather be on the spot. We've been in touch with David's parents – he's the friend Peter was to meet in Zermatt. They don't know exactly where their son is, but they think he was expecting Peter too. We'll be going to London this evening. There's a plane at nine thirty-five tomorrow which gets us to Geneva at five past twelve. Is there any easy way of getting from Geneva to Chamonix?'

There isn't. I assured her I had no special plans and would be happy to come and meet them. I could do it in an hour on the motorway, and I'd be glad to spare Lady Westmorland a little fatigue. This last argument decided her daughter in favour of the idea. She told me where to reach them in London in case there was any more news between now and next day, and gave me the number of their flight, which I still remember: Swissair 831. I had only too clear an idea of what they would be feeling about their journey, and I didn't know what it would be best to say in the way of optimism and encouragement. I said something, anyway, and we rang off.

I couldn't settle to work. Late that afternoon, after sorting out my equipment and tidying my books and papers, I decided to go over to the camp the English climbers used.

The uninitiated don't know it, but this place is one of the most picturesque spots in a valley which can boast of many such. Tents of every kind are pitched here amidst an amazing jumble of stretchers and pegs, from the latest model designed for the Himalayas to items from American army surplus stores. The best and youngest climbers of the British Isles stay here, crowds of them: working men from Wales, undergraduates from Oxford and Cambridge. It is a place where remarkable climbs have taken place over the years, and the mountaineers who have made them return modestly to it. But remarkable as this shrine to mountaineering may be, when British climbers get a bit older and have rather more money, they often prefer to abandon the fraternal promiscuity of the camp site for a little more rustic solitude. I love the English camp site, I often go there, but I wasn't at all surprised that Peter

Westmorland had chosen to pitch his tent somewhere quieter. All the same, I could hope to find help here, and perhaps even useful information. Sure enough, I'd hardly arrived when I spotted Simon Richardson and Nick Barrett, two young climbers I knew very well. I told them about our problem. They promised to pass the news around the camp, so that their friends would tell them about any contact they'd had with Peter Westmorland, or any traces he might have left in a mountain hut.

By next morning the situation had developed no further. No news, certainly, but no bad news either. Seeing that I had taken charge and the family were coming, Robert and Étienne decided to go climbing again. Myself, I drove down to Geneva in that state of uncertainty you feel when you're afraid of having given way to anxiety too soon, and perhaps inconsiderately communicating it to others. At the airport, I also regretted not finding out what the people I'd come to meet looked like. There was a crowd, and several planes must have landed almost at the same time. The passengers were coming through two doors about fifteen metres apart which I couldn't watch simultaneously, and the arrivals board had been showing that the London flight was in for some time as I continued shuttling between them, looking for bags carrying a Heathrow label and scrutinizing the women travellers in vain. Time passed, and I was wondering if there'd been some inexplicable mistake and I'd have to leave alone. Then, suddenly, I felt sure I'd spotted the couple I was expecting. Their faces did not, like those of so many others, wear the busy, cheerful expression of holiday-makers; you could see deep internal tension beneath their composed serenity. In spite of her drawn features, Lady Westmorland was still very beautiful. Even without a reason like mine to take an interest in her, you couldn't help noticing her tall, supple figure, well dressed in a beige suit with matching handbag and shoes, and a light hat on her wavy grey hair. She had an unusually elegant way of carrying her head, and a very sweet expression which further emphasized the kindness of her eyes. Her daughter was like her, although not so tall and less thin, with an almost childish look. I thought she couldn't be twenty yet, but I found out later that she was nearly twenty-four. She was wearing an almond-green outfit which brought out her clear complexion, golden chestnut hair and grey eyes. Although she could hardly have slept the night before either, she was making a great effort to look cheerful, and showed loving, anxious solicitude for her mother. I went up to them; we hardly needed to introduce ourselves. Lady Westmorland thanked me, apologized for the trouble she was giving me, and talked to me, smiling, about her son.

All the way back I kept admiring the control both women exerted over anxiety that had been serious enough to make them set out at once. They took great pains to put me at my ease, and personally I thought of nothing but restoring their peace of mind and pointing out that we had no real cause for alarm, since no accident had been reported in a massif which was frequented everywhere by a great many climbers. I tried to encourage them, assuring them that I'd almost certainly decided to let them know too soon, and citing similar cases where strong reasons for anxiety had eventually turned out groundless, and there was a perfectly rational explanation for someone's absence or delay. Finally, I emphasized the fact that the weather had been remarkably settled over the last week.

As we approached Sallanches I left the motorway so that we could have lunch before entering the Chamonix valley, where new worries were bound to occur to the two women. They wanted to know just how I'd heard about Peter myself, and all about the enquiries I'd made yesterday and the day before. When I told them how I had discovered that Peter and I were working in very similar fields, he in archaeology and I in history, and how we were both very interested in Oman, they were amazed by the coincidence of our having so much in common. But whenever there was a pause in the conversation, I could feel his mother's attention straying away from me and taking an anxious direction once more. Then, with the girl's help, I tried to get the talk going again and made confident remarks designed to show how ordinary life and happiness were bound to triumph over the vague threat of the unknown. Dorothy Westmorland found a photograph of Peter in her bag to show me. I liked the look of the young man at once: I liked his determined appearance, straight gaze and humorous smile. I heard all sorts of interesting details about him, and we made plans for all four of us to meet again once we had found Peter.

As I had foreseen, anxiety gained the upper hand when we reached Chamonix. I accompanied Lady Westmorland and her daughter to the mountain rescue station, where we gave official notice of Peter's possible disappearance. I realized that my companions understood French and even spoke it very correctly. The gendarme who explained the near impossibility of a search, given no clue at all as to location, was also reassuring, so far as there was nothing to suggest that Peter's absence was really unusual. Then I found the two women a hotel, made sure they had all they needed, left them my address, advised them to get some rest and finally said goodbye, after we had sent telegrams which might help to clarify the situation to Zermatt. After that I went back to Peter's tent on my own once more, dreaming of finding him back there and taking him to his family. But it was just the same as before, and I merely left a message there.

I felt optimistic that evening, having remembered a similar incident when everyone had been very worried about a young man who, as we learned a little later, was happily doing the Tour du Mont Blanc with a girl-friend at the time. Peter's absence could have an equally simple and commonplace reason, even if we couldn't guess what it was just now.

Next day, the 17th, passed without any news either good or bad to provide more information. I spent a great deal of time with Lady Westmorland and her daughter, still admiring their dignity and their concern for the trouble they might be giving other people, while they kept their own reasons for anxiety to themselves. Despite everything, I wasn't really worried myself, and much of my confidence must have been because I felt sure I'd soon be meeting Peter Westmorland at last. I was also sure of the pleasure such a meeting would give me, and the friendship bound to develop between us.

But everything was changed by three successive incidents. First came the bad weather: an unexpected storm which broke on the night of the 17th. It kept me awake for hours on end, thinking of the women who, a prey to their dual solitude and their fears, must be asking question after question that couldn't be answered. In the morning Chamonix was enveloped in a grey drizzle which went on all day, distilling impalpable anxiety about the fate of anyone who might be trapped at high altitude by the storm. It had turned cold, and it must be snowing up on the mountains. Then Dave Sykes arrived: one of our telegrams had reached him, and he told us he was surprised Peter had failed to turn up in Zermatt and hadn't let him know in advance either: that wasn't his style. Finally, towards evening, an English climbing party coming down from the Eccles bivouac hut told us they had found information that Peter Westmorland and an American called Bryan Marks had been at Monzino on July 10th and Eccles on the 11th, and had set out from there to do the Innominata. After that, all hope seemed lost, for although there are records of a mountaineer being rescued after a week in a crevasse, that remains an exceptional case. Anyway, it was more than a week now, and the bad weather seemed to make searching that dangerous and distant sector impossible.

I shall never forget Lady Westmorland's grief: she was so calm, silent and cold, keeping it all to herself. We wished she would weep and sob, let it all out, but she was like a statue frozen in her sorrow, emerging from it occasionally only to worry about the rescue team; she didn't want them taking risks when she knew there was no chance of success. She and her daughter left a few days later, asking me to sort out Peter's things and bring them the most personal on one of my next visits to England, giving the rest to other British climbers. So I gave away his tent, his sleeping bag, some clothes, some minor pieces of equipment, and as a souvenir of friendship I kept his Vallot guides and a karabiner marked with his initials for myself.

The bodies of Bryan Marks and Peter were never found. No doubt they lie buried in a crevasse of the upper Brouillard Glacier. I kept Lady Westmorland informed about the progress of the searches, and told her in October that as I had to visit London soon I was thinking of dropping in to see her at Widecombe, bringing Peter's personal papers, which were still in my hands. Dorothy Westmorland told me that her mother was ill, but if I ever had time and opportunity they'd be very glad if I would agree to look through Peter's files, perhaps get what he had been working on published, and give his books and documents to specialist libraries. They were only afraid of asking me to shoulder too heavy a burden, and hoped I would give them a frank reply. In fact I was very happy to accept. Other researchers could of course have done the job just as well, but I was touched that the family turned to me because I'd been involved in the aftermath of the accident and felt really drawn to the dead man. It's a fact that I felt so close to him I couldn't put him out of my mind all the rest of that season, and when Serge came back we even climbed the Innominata Ridge in the hope of finding some clue or last memento.

I had my Christmas holidays free, and it was understood that I would spend two weeks at Kermist Hall. That was when I really got to know Peter. I found the house very much as I'd imagined it that July morning when I first phoned. It was spacious, although now too empty, both comfortable and full of those draughts inseparable from the British idea of good health. Deep in a valley that was still green, with a stream of water running through it, it was not far from the moors, where the storm wind blew over bare rocks, short grass, furze and faded heather.

Peter's room had been left just as it was. Every day, for hours on end, I classified his papers, making my way with increasing emotion into his innermost thoughts and a mind which I found very much in tune with my own. There was an article on the Sohar site, nearly completed, and a book more than three-quarters finished with enough additional notes to enable it to be completed for purposes of publication. And then I found notebooks of personal writings, adolescent poems, letters, humorous climbing tales. Gradually I uncovered the life and the soul of a man I had never known: it was the kind of opportunity one very seldom has.

I used to start work very early in the morning, and apart from a short break for lunch I went on until about four or five. Then we met for tea around a glowing fire. The sound of the wind blowing outside accentuated the charm of the setting, the delicacy of the old embossed teapot, the bone china cups, the plates of golden scones and crumpets, the bowl of thick cream we spread on them. I would tell Lady Westmorland and her daughter what I had found that day, explained the scientific conclusions to be drawn from it, and showed them the writings which had moved me most. I think it made it easier for them to encounter the dead man like that, through a stranger with whom they had to restrain the emotions they would have felt if they themselves were sorting out their son's and brother's papers.

After tea I went out walking for an hour or so on the dark moor, buffeted by gusts of wind, gales and rain, before coming back, shivering, to the big, welcoming house. We dined early and always ended the evening talking at length about Peter, his childhood, his studies, his travels, his favourite subjects, just as if he were still there with us. I ought to point out that there was nothing excessive or morbid about these conversations; quite the reverse. It was the living presence of Peter that animated us: his mind, his cheerfulness, the passionate attention he brought to everything. I've met a great many men in my time, but I am sure I've never known any of them as deeply and intimately as my unknown friend, Peter Westmorland.

Several years have passed since all this happened, and life has brought its usual succession of vicissitudes, cares and joys. And yet the memory of that July evening when it all began is as vivid in my mind as ever. I got Peter's last article published in the influential journal *Der Islam*, and I also made sure his book was published, adding a biographical note on the author and an introduction explaining how it was that I had been called in make the final revisions. I don't climb as much as I used to because of my new professional and family responsibilities, but we spend every summer in Chamonix in my old flatlet, now extended by the purchase of the property next door. That's where I am writing these lines in the quiet of the night, in front of a window open to show a view of the Aiguilles. I must go to Geneva airport early tomorrow morning to meet Lady Westmorland, who is coming to spend August here and meet her first grandson, whom we have of course called after his uncle, Peter, my unknown brother-in-law.

THE GAME OF MOUNTAIN AND CHANCE

Jacques Ville and Rémi Lesparrou came across each other one July 16th, at forty-three minutes past ten in the morning, in the middle of that road in Chamonix which separates the Laydernier Bank from the Piot Pharmacy. As it was over two years since they had last met, they greeted each other warmly and began to exchange news. Rémi had just finished his military service abroad, and Jacques now had a son born eighteen months ago. Having arrived by train the previous evening, Rémi was camping near the Pierre à l'Orthaz. Jacques, who had been on holiday for two weeks, had rented the little chalet on the outskirts of the village of Les Pècles where he usually spent the month of July.

The hostile reactions of various irate drivers interrupted the two friends' conversation and drove them to seek refuge on the pavement.

'Fantastic weather!' said Jacques.

'Been climbing?' enquired Rémi.

'Hardly at all,' replied Jacques. 'We've been having a lot of rain.'

'What are conditions like in the mountains?'

'You can see for yourself! The rock's not dry yet, but it seems the snow's excellent. I had that from Bruno, who did the Gervasutti Couloir yesterday. I was hoping to get up there before the conditions deteriorated.'

'Who are you climbing with?' asked Rémi.

'No one in particular,' said Jacques. 'Depends on chance and who I come across.'

'Well, this is a lucky chance, then!' said Rémi. 'I came into town to find a climbing partner, and I'd like to do the Gervasutti myself.'

'Great!' said Jacques. 'It'd be good to be in the mountains with you again. Let's go up this evening and do the route tomorrow.'

'Fine!' said Rémi. 'So what gear do we need? I have a rope which ... '

'Let's discuss all that a little later, if you don't mind,' said Jacques. 'I have to post a registered letter, get some money out of the bank and buy a paper. It's five past eleven; say that takes me twenty minutes or so. Meet you here again at eleven-thirty and we'll fix everything, okay?'

Jacques began at the savings bank. He was not the only person with business there, and had to wait longer than he had expected, first at the counter and then at the cash withdrawal point. He took it philosophically. But when he came out he noticed that the church clock already said eleven twenty-two, and made haste to the post office. It was full; in fact its population density per square metre was at maximum capacity. Of the two counter positions designated for the operation Jacques intended to perform, one was closed and the other unattended. Meanwhile, Jacques saw that the queue which he had joined consisted of fourteen patient sufferers, some of them sunk in the final depths of despair.

'Has the counter clerk been gone long?' Jacques asked the old gentleman in front of him.

'No idea,' sighed the old gentleman. 'There wasn't anyone there when I arrived. But the queue does move now and then, because sometimes people give up.'

Wishing he had bought his newspaper first, Jacques closed his eyes and tried to forget the depressing atmosphere of the queue by absorbing himself in the thought of the sunlit, snowy spaces where he would be tomorrow.

By the time he was finally outside again, it was a quarter to twelve.

'Oh blast it', he said to himself. 'Rémi hasn't waited for me. Where's the sod got to?'

Scanning his surroundings to no avail, he decided to try the nearest cafés.

The fact was that Rémi hadn't even arrived yet, which was not entirely his fault.

Since he had a little time to kill, he had decided to go to Snell's to buy some gaiters. On the way, outside Trimaille the jeweller's, he met Pierre.

'What a surprise!' he exclaimed. 'I'm running into all my old friends. What news since I last saw you?'

'You know François is dead, I expect?' asked Pierre.

'Good heavens, no! That's dreadful. How did it happen?'

'Wind slab,' Pierre told him, soberly. 'He was climbing with Laurent. Laurent died too last year. What else ...? Oh, yes, Ludovic! Stupidly unroping himself at a belay in the Petites Jorasses. He was lucky to get away with no worse than a cracked skull. Then last March, Philippe and Luc were skiing off piste and set off an avalanche. Ten broken ribs, one crushed vertebra. Let's see ... this summer two blokes fell in the Aiguille du Goûter couloir, and ... '

'Thanks for getting me into the feel of things again, mate!' Rémi interrupted. 'Very kind of you. Thanks again, but that'll have to do for now. 'Scuse me, I have some shopping to do.'

In Snell's he met Mathieu and discussed conditions in the mountains with him before choosing his gaiters. Then he went to the Maison de la Presse to buy his parents a reassuring postcard showing nothing but rhododendrons. Coming out, he saw Valentine Grove, who was looking at a pair of candlesticks on display in Madame Lavaivre's window.

'Valentine!' cried Rémi. 'Chamonix is really amazing! As soon as you arrive you meet all your old friends. I've already run into Jacques and Pierre, and I left Mathieu only a moment ago.'

'You know he's not with Coralie any more?' said Valentine.

'Really? We didn't get round to that. Well, well! So he and Coralie aren't together now?'

'No,' Valentine confirmed. 'Coralie's with Georges, who left Danielle, and Mathieu is with Cécile, after a bit of a fling with Brigitte, now I come to think of it ... because Brigitte has split up with Jean, who's with Juliette now, after Juliette was really depressed over Frédéric, who chucked her for Nathalie when Nathalie had given Marc the push. You mean you didn't know? A real drama! Then there's Robert, who left Estelle a good six months ago, and according to what Chantal told me Estelle has moved in with Alexandre. Let's see ... Delphine's not with Michel any more, but that was always on the cards! Stéphane has left Antoinette ... '

'Look, why not tell me who *are* still together?' suggested Rémi ingeniously. 'It'll be quicker that way!'

'Right. Well ... wait, I think Odile is still with Henri-Jean!'

'Well, that's a relief!' said Rémi. 'You never know what's been happening while you're away, and it's so easy to drop a brick. Thanks for the social column! Now, I have to go, I think I'm late.'

But having then run into Nicolas, who was keen to impart every detail of the climb he had done the day before, and thereafter, even more unexpectedly, having met his grandmother's next-door neighbour, a lady who was astonished by this coincidence and wanted him to stop and tell her about the cave on the Les Bossons Glacier, Rémi did not reach the meeting place until ten to twelve, and failed to find Jacques there.

'The idiot!' thought Rémi. 'He might have waited for me. Where do I look for him now, I wonder?'

Jacques had gone off towards the Brasserie Centrale, where he saw no familiar faces and went on his way straight to the Landru bookshop to buy his newspaper, scrutinizing the terrace of the Irish Coffee shop in passing, and stopping for a moment for a little chat with Serge and Julien.

Then he went into the bookshop. He bought *Le Dauphiné*, glanced at the mountaineering books, remembered that he needed some envelopes, passed the time of day with Madame Collignon, and paid for his purchases. On coming out he almost crashed into Patrice and Gilles, who happened to be passing, and asked whether they had by any chance seen Rémi. When they answered in the negative, he decided to pursue his researches at the weather bureau.

'You're getting warm!' cried Destiny.

But Jacques did not hear. He conceived the unfortunate notion of going along the Rue de l'Hôtel-de-Ville and the dark little alley just off it.

The notion was unfortunate because after inspecting the terrace of the Potinière and the interior of the Bar National, going to the tobacconist's for cigarettes, and then walking back up the Passage du Bartavel, Rémi had decided to consult the latest weather forecast, had met René at the weather bureau, exchanged a few words with him, and was just coming back down to the centre and passing the front of the Town Hall as his friend was passing the back of it.

So it was not surprising that Jacques failed to meet Rémi. However, in his own turn he met René.

'Haven't seen Rémi, have you?' he asked.

'He left me a moment ago!' exclaimed René.

'Oh no!' sighed Jacques. 'What bad luck! We were supposed to meet an hour ago, and now I can't find him anywhere!'

'He was looking for you too,' René confirmed. 'I think he went that way.'

Jacques and Rémi continued their fruitless search for half an hour. As Jacques turned into the arcades of the Avenue Michel-Croz, Rémi was walking down the Arve in front of the Casino. And when he was going along the Rue Vallot, his friend was coming up the Rue Paccard.

Jacques was the first to get tired of it. When one o'clock struck, he remembered that his wife would be expecting him for lunch, went back to his car and drove off. There was no hurry, he told himself. Plenty of time to go to the Pierre à l'Orthaz and find Rémi early in the afternoon.

Unaware that there was no longer any point in his search, Rémi went on with it for another ten minutes. Then, meeting Lucile, who was on her way to the Choucas with some friends, he joined the group, had a very pleasant lunch with them, said goodbye to them all at two o'clock and strode off towards Les Pècles.

At twelve minutes past two, Jacques told his wife Corinne that he must go and look for Rémi.

'Do something for me, will you?' she asked. 'Can you go by way of Les Gaillands and the main road? You could look in at Claude's and leave a book I promised to lend him. And you won't forget to mend the baby's cot before tonight, will you?'

'No problem,' said Jacques.

The only problem, though he could not know it, was that in going into town by the lower road he would miss Rémi, who was coming along the higher road.

'Isn't Jacques here?' said Rémi in surprise, when he reached the chalet.

'Didn't you meet him?' said Corinne. 'What bad luck! He's just left to go and look for you. You'd better wait here. He'll have to come back when he doesn't find you.'

Jacques had thought he would have no difficulty in locating Rémi's tent, but when he reached the camp site he realized that the task was going to be harder than he expected. The Pierre à l'Orthaz site was covered with tents, and Rémi was quite likely to be camping on his own somewhere nearby; that would be just his style. Jacques searched for some time, questioned several people, and suddenly had an intuition: his friend, on the same errand, must be back at his own place.

Sure enough, at that moment Rémi was indeed still there. But when Jérôme dropped in and suggested driving him back to his tent, he decided to take advantage of the offer, leaving precise directions about his whereabouts with Corinne.

The two cars took the Route Blanche, passing each other fast at eighteen minutes past three.

Back at Les Pècles, Jacques was torn between his impatience at this new contretemps and the relief of knowing that his wanderings were over. He set off again almost at once. At quarter to four the two men were finally reunited.

'Get changed, quick,' said Jacques. 'And pack your sack! We still

have to go back to my place so I can get ready. And we must buy food.
Bring all your stuff! We can sort it out later.'

'There's no mad rush!' Rémi protested.

'No, but all the same ... the last téléphérique must be at six. I haven't
had time to check.'

'It was running until almost nine last night' Rémi assured him.

'Yes, but bringing tourists down. They don't take people up to the
Aiguille at that time of day.'

'I'll get ready,' said Rémi, suiting the action to the word.

To get back to Les Pècles, Jacques drove over the Plaine des Praz and
took the Nants road. When he found himself near the Brévent cable car
station, he thought it would be wise to do their shopping while they
were near the centre. He drove down the Mollard to the car park near
the church, but it was full, so he parked outside the presbytery garage.

'I'll stay in the car in case I need to move it,' he told Rémi. 'You go
and buy what we need from Mesdemoiselles Gilloz, and don't dawdle!'

However, Jacques's wait went on for ever. Several times he was
about to leave his car, and decided not to in case he missed his friend.
He was in a very bad temper when Rémi got back.

'I don't believe it!' he grumbled, switching on the ignition. 'What on
earth have you been doing?'

'Looking for bread,' confessed Rémi. 'Sorry, but I really can't do
without bread. And the place was very crowded, so it took time.'

They drove back to Les Pècles fast. Jacques changed, packed his
sack, and began sorting the equipment, dividing it between himself and
Rémi.

'You won't forget about the baby's cot, will you?' said Corinne.

'Oh no!' sighed Jacques.

'Can't it wait till tomorrow?' asked Rémi.

'You're not the one sleeping in it!' replied Jacques briefly, going to
fetch his tools.

The repair took a few minutes, and then, finally, the two mountaineers
set off. They reached the Aiguille du Midi cable car station at three
minutes to five, had some difficulty in finding a parking place, took their
rucksacks and ice axes out of the boot, and went into the station.

'Two returns for the Midi, please!' asked Jacques.

'The last cabin's just left!' replied the ticket clerk cheerfully.

'I don't believe it!' fulminated Jacques. 'It's hardly five o'clock yet!'

'It's left, all the same, like I said,' confirmed the clerk, sorting out his till. 'It's after five. Not long after, no, but the last cabin leaves at five.'

'Can't we take the next one? We thought there was another at six.'

'Sure you did! It's the same every evening, if that's any consolation, but what do you expect me to do? I don't draw up the timetable, you know. And standing about here won't get you anywhere.'

Jacques and Rémi looked at each other with hostile disappointment.

'And it's too late to try going up on the Italian side,' said Jacques.

'Why not a different climb, starting in the morning?' suggested Rémi.

'Don't feel like it,' said Jacques. 'I wanted to do the Gervasutti. I certainly shan't forget today in a hurry. Well, pick your sack up and I'll drive you back.'

The two men parted without goodwill.

'Back already?' one of Rémi's neighbours asked him.

'Yes,' grunted Rémi. 'A real cock-up! We missed the last cable. The friend I was supposed to be going with went missing all day, and then at the last minute he had to waste time mending his kid's cot. And this is the result! Fine start to my holiday, I must say!'

'You're back?' said Corinne, surprised.

'Let's not discuss it!' said Jacques. 'The last cable left before our eyes. Not only have I spent a whole day chasing about after Rémi, if that fool hadn't wasted ten minutes looking for bread we'd easily have made it. Such a good climb – and with the weather like this! Hey, ask Charlotte if she can baby-sit this evening. We'll have dinner at the Fouffion, and then I'll feel better. But I won't forget bad luck like this in a hurry!'

Life is full of surprises. Jacques and Rémi, who thought they would never get over the disappointment of missing that last cable, had no difficulty in doing so next day, when they heard that the séracs which broke away from the top of the Gervasutti Couloir at six fifty-seven in the morning had swept away all six mountaineers who were spaced out along the slope and who, had chance not intervened, would have been not six but eight.

SOMETHING THAT COULD BE
AN OLD MOUNTAIN LEGEND

Long, long ago, in an Alpine valley, there lived a guide who was the honour, glory and ornament of his profession. Ever brave, ever cheerful, the best man you could find to scale a difficult rock pitch, even better at cutting good steps up a couloir of ice to give his client an easy ascent. Then there was his skill in judging the nature of the terrain, choosing the right routes, spotting dangers, assessing conditions, and knowing more than anyone, particularly our modern meteorologists, what next day's weather would be like.

This remarkable man was called Agapit Trévillaz, and all the good clients of the time, English gentlemen in particular, used to try to obtain his services, offering a very high fee. But Agapit Trévillaz was not a mercenary character. What mattered to him was being able to choose his companions, rather than giving preference to those whose pockets were well lined. He wanted to complete the best climbs successfully and safely, and then in autumn go quietly back to his old family farm, his beloved wife and his brood of children, see to the fields and the livestock, help the neighbours who had helped him out themselves during the season, and on winter evenings he liked to sit by the fire and think of the climbs to come.

Agapit Trévillaz was well aware of his merits and could not have borne to see anyone cast doubt on them. Going one better than Ravanel le Rouge who, having climbed with a king, was described as 'the guide of kings and king of guides', Agapit, who had been mule driver to an emperor in his youth, cheerfully called himself 'the guide of emperors and emperor of guides', and indeed would have been happy with a yet more glorious title to describe the nature of his exploits. To put it in a nutshell, he lacked modesty to such an extent that a certain irritation about it began to be felt, even beyond the pearly gates.

I should say here that Agapit Trévillaz had an unusual first name which was quite a story in itself. One day his grandfather the pedlar, while on the road, had met a girl from Néfiach. Néfiach was a parish in Roussillon, and St Agapit was its patron saint. The young people fell in love and married, but the lovely Lydia, unused to the rigours of the Alpine winter and nostalgic for her Catalan homeland, had vowed at the very beginning of her marriage to call her first-born son after the patron saint of Néfiach. Successive additions to the family hearth were an Agathe, an Alphonsine, an Albine, an Alice, an Aline and an Adolphine ... but no boys at all! It was not until Alphonsine married one Léon Trévillaz that the first grandson could be given the venerated name of Agapit.

All this is more important than it may seem, since Agapit Trévillaz's unusual first name proved a real bonus. His patron saint was not exactly overworked, like St. Peter or St. John, for instance, always snowed under with other people's business. St. Agapit had plenty of time on his hands, and he did a conscientious job. As Néfiach did not give him too much trouble, he was able to keep a watchful eye on those few individuals recommended to his care. And among those, he would have felt a particular affection for Agapit Trévillaz had that gentleman shown a little more humility.

St. Agapit worked like the devil, if one may so put it, for the good of Agapit Trévillaz. He had private conversations with Agapit's personal guardian angel, issuing him with the firmest of instructions. He consulted experienced colleagues. And finally, not knowing where to turn next, he asked God for an audience.

'Dear God!' he begged. 'Holy Trinity! Take a look at the mess poor Agapit Trévillaz's soul is getting into there below! In these troubled times, when evil is so rampant, here's a just, upright, honest man, cheerful, a good worker, a good husband and father, in fact someone endowed with all the qualities you could hope for in a mortal man. He could have been a second St. Agapit, but he won't! There he goes spoiling everything by telling himself he's the best guide in the world! The best! We'll soon see if he's the best when he's climbing the incandescent bitumen of Hell! The fact is, I've tried everything, and nothing worked. Only You, Almighty, can do anything to help that pigheaded fellow!'

So the Holy Ghost, who always gets good ideas, hummed a little tune like an inspiration, and Our Lord Jesus Christ said to his Father, 'I'm sure something can be done. It so happens that Agapit Trévillaz is going to lose his porter, who is deciding at this very moment to marry a girl in another village and go into his future father-in-law's business. The season's about to begin, and Agapit will be in real trouble. I feel a certain urge to pay another little visit to Earth ... '

Real trouble was certainly the way to describe Agapit's predicament. No porter, at the last minute! And nothing he could say would persuade that stubborn Isidore to climb for one more season. He approached various young fellows, and none of them would do for him. They all asked stupid questions:

'Not too tiring, is it?'

'Not too dangerous, is it?'

'Is the pay good?'

None of them, absolutely none, had any feeling or liking for the mountains. His own sons were still much too young, and the clients would soon be arriving.

Then, one fine morning, when Agapit was mowing outside his farm, a tall young man came along the road. A well-built young man, with a frank, open face and a huge smile.

'Morning, Père Trévillaz!' he said with great composure. 'I'm told you're looking for a porter.'

'A porter! You're a gift from God!' sighed Agapit, with no idea how right he was. 'Oh yes, I most certainly am looking for a porter! Ever done the job before?'

'No,' admitted the handsome young man, honestly.

'What's your trade, then?'

'I used to be a carpenter,' replied the young man.

'Carpenters are all right by me,' Agapit Trévillaz assured him. 'They're good workers, they don't shirk on the job. I like you! What's your name?'

'They call my name Emmanuel,' replied Our Lord, for as you will have guessed, it was He.

'Right, Emmanuel, it's a bargain! I'll have to take you on trial, of course, but I have every confidence in you. And to be frank, you'll be learning the job with the best guide who could possibly teach you! The very best of the best, and I can say so without boasting!'

The first clients were just arriving, and Agapit Trévillaz decided to take a gentleman from Paris up the Pic des Vents first. It was quite an easy climb, but a long and varied one. The guide gave his porter a heavily loaded bag to carry, to see how he worked, and kept a close eye on him as they climbed.

There was no fault to be found with him. He went well, just like that, from the start, almost better than the lamented Isidore. Forging straight ahead, never getting breathless, never complaining, showing no fear of the drop below, always keeping an eye on the gentleman struggling along between the two of them. And full of little attentions too! He had even decided, entirely of his own accord, to put a bottle in his sack for a nice surprise, as they found when they reached the peak and passed round the flask which Agapit himself had filled at the waterfall the night before, and which now turned out to be full of delicious white wine. A good porter if ever Agapit saw one!

Agapit Trévillaz did not hesitate, therefore, to take Emmanuel on the second climb he was planning. This was a serious one: the Aiguille Bleue. It had only ever been climbed twice before, and the first ascent had been made by Agapit Trévillaz himself. His client was an Englishman, a very strong climber, who wanted to take his guide on with him afterwards to a particularly difficult mountain, unclimbed from any side, and for good reason, although many had tried. Even its name was impressive: the Schwindelhorn!

If Emmanuel did well on the Aiguille Bleue, what a team they'd make to conquer the Schwindelhorn!

In fact Emmanuel did so well that Agapit Trévillaz began to feel very slightly irritated. It was distinctly pretentious of a young fellow like that to climb almost – almost, mark you – as well as the guide leading the climb, who was without a shadow of doubt the most extraordinary guide in any country and of any time. Imagine a porter climbing like that, first go off, without previous experience!

Agapit Trévillaz took care to give him a few instructions, playing his part as leader and master:

'Hold yourself upright in those steps, Emmanuel!'

'Remember never to linger under a sérac, my boy!'

'The rope must stay taut, never drag along the ground, so just make sure it does, young fellow!'

But this was only for something to say, since you really couldn't fault Emmanuel. He always did what needed to be done, just the way it needed to be done, and exactly when it needed to be done. Things got to the point where their client realized it, and once, hesitating slightly in a passage, he turned to the porter to ask what to do! Agapit Trévillaz had not cared for this incident at all, and he went the last hundred metres up the couloir muttering into his moustache.

They finally reached the col, separated from the summit of the Aiguille Bleue only by two or three hundred metres of ridge. The guide could not help giving vent to a bad-tempered impulse.

'You stay on the col, Emmanuel!' he ordered. 'You're still too much of a beginner to climb this ridge and the summit of the Aiguille Bleue; it's a big mountain. Unrope yourself and wait for us here.'

However, he very soon regretted these cross remarks. He was a fair man, and knew that if any porter ever deserved to climb the Aiguille Bleue it was a young fellow as gifted as Emmanuel. It had been unkind to make him stay behind and deprive him of a fine summit he might never have the chance to climb again.

Moreover, the English gentleman was beginning to tire. The ridge was extremely sharp, and it was a long job to flatten it with blows of the ice axe, trying to make the going slightly more amenable. It would have been better to keep the client in between the two of them.

Agapit Trévillaz did not linger on the summit, although it was morning and the view was so good that he had rarely seen one to equal it – and he had seen many fine views! Rocky peaks bristling below you and around you, and successive ranges of mountains building up and receding towards distant horizons, blue with mist ...

He hurried his English client along a little; the gentleman would have liked to spend longer admiring the view, but it was a good thing they did make haste, because the snow of the ridge had been quick to soften, and for safety they had to descend most of it *à cheval*.

I was really stupid, thought Agapit. I just hope Emmanuel isn't too upset at being left on that col. Or too angry either! In his place I'd have ... well, I just hope he doesn't decide to give up being a porter ...

'Come along, Mr Levington!' he said impatiently. 'Come along, we don't want to spend the night up here. Hurry up!'

He was always so calm with clients, and now here he was getting irascible, all for lack of his porter!

But once back on the col they found Emmanuel in cheerful mood, humming a little Alleluia. Not going up to the summit didn't seem to have bothered him too much. He had prepared an excellent snack, and welcomed his party back with a kindly smile.

'You can come to the Schwindelhorn with us!' Agapit immediately assured him.

However, they had to wait a while to make that ascent, because bad weather set in. For two weeks Emmanuel helped out on the farm, built up the woodpile for winter, carried Madame Trévillaz's buckets, taught the eldest children to read, played horses with the little ones, kept Mr Levington happy by showing him the attractions of gathering mushrooms, and listened with untiring goodwill to reminiscences of Agapit Trévillaz's climbs. He really was a very pleasant young man, and when the weather seemed to be improving slightly Agapit was happy to set out with him again, cheered on by the Trévillaz children, who were sure they would succeed in making the first ascent.

But they had to get going. Mr Levington could not stay more than a week longer, and in spite of the fresh snow not having melted yet, and the doubts they had about the weather, they must make the attempt. It was now or perhaps never.

The Schwindelhorn was indeed a forbidding mountain, falling steeply away on all sides, armour-plated with ice and steep slabs of rock, and high. They slept by a small blue lake called the Dohlensee, and began the climb next day. Agapit Trévillaz thought he had seen a possible route never before tried by climbers attempting to make the first ascent.

They set off in darkness, by lantern light, and spent ten hours struggling upwards. Emmanuel was a great help to his employer. You couldn't find a better man to detect a way through the rampart of defences the mountain raised, to spot the weak point in a bergschrund, the ledge system leading to another chimney, or the holds to be found in an apparently impregnable slab. They went on and on, fearing that they might suddenly come up against a final, insoluble problem. But suddenly there was nothing left in front of the rope but a long ridge bristling with gendarmes and snow-covered cornices which they could not fail to negotiate. The weather was certainly getting stormy. The air was heavy, and great dark clouds were gathering in the west. However, their goal was very close now, and none of the three men would have dreamt of renouncing certain victory. Soon they were all joyfully embracing each other on the narrow snowy peak. They had conquered the Schwindelhorn!

Now they had to get back down again. As expected, the weather had turned nasty. A storm broke, violent and brief, but leaving the mountain covered with sleet and swathed in a thick blanket of cloud from which snow went on falling. Agapit tried to get his bearings as best he could on this new mountain, where he lacked any landmarks.

'Left! Over to the left more!' he shouted to his porter, who was climbing down in front, while he himself ensured the team's stability at the back.

'But Père Trévillaz,' protested Emmanuel, 'we'd be making for the North Face.'

'Do as I tell you, greenhorn!' growled Agapit, who was not used to having his authority challenged, particularly in front of a client. 'Over to the left more!'

And of course it happened. They soon found themselves on increasingly steep slopes, slopes which Emmanuel, luckily, could cut properly. Then they suddenly came up against a huge crevasse or bergschrund, reaching as far as the eye could see, and wider than you'd have thought possible. It was one of the kind you could make out clearly from below as interruptions in the slope of the North Face. There was no way across it, since the fragile arch of ice which connected the two lips over a distance of nearly nine metres could hardly even be described as a snow bridge. Nor could it possibly be jumped. And between the edges of the bergschrund lay a great void with shining, overhanging, blue-tinged walls. They would have to climb all the way back up again, however tired they were, and then search once more, try to get their bearings and bivouac heaven only knew where, in clothes now stiffening with frost. And then what? For the first time in his life, Agapit Trévillaz really felt fear.

'I'll go over the arch,' suggested Emmanuel.

'Are you crazy?' growled Agapit. 'It wouldn't bear the weight of a cat! We must go back up.'

'It'll be all right, you'll see,' replied Emmanuel. 'There's a knack to doing these things. Watch me!'

And his feet gently gliding, moving so lightly he did not seem to be touching the ground, Emmanuel delicately crossed the bridge and secured the rope on the other side. On his own side, Agapit quickly dug an anchor point out of the ice, sent his client down on the rope, keeping him steady on the other strand, and when his turn came he hung from the double rope by his wrists, got to the other side and hauled it in. It had been a remarkable feat.

They could now go on down, wholly bent on getting lower and escaping the snares of the mountain and the blizzard as fast as possible.

But then, a little later, they reached another bergschrund, as deep and wide and long as the first. It stretched on and on. Once again a slender bridge of ice joined the two sides in a curious spidery arch.

'I'll go across,' said Emmanuel.

'Oh no you won't!' growled Trévillaz, not wishing to appear less competent than his porter. 'I've never needed to use this technique before, but I know it so well in principle that makes no difference, and I can do it as well as you can! Just watch the rope!'

And Agapit began gliding his feet over the arch of ice. He soon felt sorry he had succumbed to vanity rather than sending his porter across.

It must hold, it had to hold ... He was thinner and more wiry than Emmanuel, and this bridge was a little less fragile than the first. All the same, he broke out into a sweat of anxiety as he thought of the icy chasms above which he was walking, supported only by this thin arch of frozen water. Well, it just wouldn't go, so that was that!

'Oh Christ all-bloody-mighty!' he muttered desperately into his moustache.

And then he felt his foot slip on the surface of the ice, and he fell. He had already gone five or six metres over the bridge, so his violent fall was also five or six metres before he struck the upper wall of the bergschrund and dangled pitifully at the end of the rope, under an overhang, bruised, bleeding and humiliated.

Fortunately Emmanuel was able to take charge of the climb from that point on. He hauled his employer back up, patched up the damage, went over the ice bridge himself, made sure the rest of the team got across, and found his way through the cluster of séracs and crevasses they then had to negotiate. Late that evening, the three men reached the upper Alpine meadows and camped there for the night. But Agapit must have been suffering from his injuries, for Emmanuel frequently heard him sighing heavily.

'You want to leave me?' Agapit Trévillaz asked his porter a few days later. 'With ability like yours? And think of the career you could have ahead of you! Anyway, what will I do without you?'

'But I've found you another porter!' repeated Emmanuel. 'I have business in the country, and here's Anatole, just back from his military service. He's young, strong and agile. You'll train him ...'

'Train him, train him ... oh yes, of course!' sighed Trévillaz. 'If that's it, then, I'll train you as best I can, young Anatole. For a start, I'll teach you something I believe is central to everything else: we don't amount to much! But at least we must do what we can with the poor means at our disposal, and do it with all our heart.'

So that is how and why Our Lord was the first to climb a certain Alpine peak. If you consult the topographical guides to the area, you will read that the first ascent of the Schwindelhorn was made by Sir Edward Levington, with the guide Agapit Trévillaz and a porter. But words do not always tell the whole story ...

THE STUNT

'Must find something to do,' grumbled Meriadoc.

'Yes, but what?' droned Ethelbert.

'Dunno, you're the clever one. Use your brains. I just can't think in this heat.'

It really was very hot. The needle on the barometer had reached the second "R" in "Very Dry" and, something that had never happened before, a family of marmots had been seen coming down from the Charlanon screes to cool off in the swimming-pool. The snow and ice was melting so fast that Wilfrid, Meriadoc's great rival, had just succeeded in making the first sail board descent of Mont Blanc.

Mariadoc hadn't thought of that one in time. 'You know,' he reminded Ethelbert, 'you know that my publisher insists that I get myself mentioned three times in the press before the book comes out.'

'I'm *so* sorry for you! There can't be many lads who have been asked to write their memoirs before they are twenty-one. What about the descent of the couloir of the Tour des Courtes by kayak? There were two dailies that put you on their front pages for that.'

'Three,' Meriadoc corrected him. 'But there was one article I didn't care for. The one where it said that we were nothing but a bunch of posers who thought only about keeping fit and training for success. I know we do 250 pull-ups on one finger every morning before even going for a slash, but we know about the pleasures of life as well as anyone else. We know about what its like to have a good blow-out on yoghurt!'

'Quite right,' agreed Ethelbert, his eyes suddenly gleaming with greed. 'But never mind what they say. The main thing is that they should talk about you. After all, you have made lots of first ascents this summer, both on the cliffs and in the mountains – nothing less that grade 7c and 8. Let's see ... there was "Nietzsche's Nick", and then "No Edelweiss for Mrs Wilkinson". And "Saussure's Assassination". And don't forget "Another One Edlinger Won't Get".'

'But the papers didn't even mention them, there are so many new routes being done nowadays. What I need is one really big success, and quick.'

'Suppose you did something funny', suggested Ethelbert, 'eye-catching of course but entirely comic. Say a first ascent on the S.S.E. face of the buttress of Gendarme 3876, wearing flippers and a diving mask.

You could call it the "Saint Tropez Gendarme". Imagine the headline: "So hot in the Alps that climbers think they are on the *Côte d'Azur*." The mask would be a bit of a nuisance, but not too much. And there ought to be enough room under the flippers for the edge of a climbing boot to stick out. I'm sure its possible. Are you listening?'

' So that's the best you can do. What a lot of crap,' sneered Meriadoc. 'Know what I think? I think it would look just a *little* bit phoney!'

'So, what about a ski descent of a completely rocky face? That hasn't been done yet. Say the West Face of the Dru! Why not? And you could get the whole thing filmed at the same time!'

'Useless – all that skiing nonsense is old hat. You could ski down an overhang, and it wouldn't surprise anyone these days. As for the West Face, even on a monoski ...'

'Stuff you then! . . . I don't know what else to suggest. Perhaps you could beat the endurance record for the Rubik Cube standing in an étrier? You could do that on the side of the Midi so the journalists could watch."

'But I don't know how to do the Rubik Cube.'

'That's the whole point, Dumbo! If you did, it would be over too quickly. With a bit of luck you might get into *The Guinness Book of Records.*'

'Naa . . . that's daft.'

'Then there are only those three other possibilities that I told you about. The Frêney Pillar in 59 minutes . . .'

'So what's new?'

'OK. What about something on the North Face of the Goûter where the rock is so rotten that there are hardly any routes.'

'Bloody ridiculous!'

'Well then, you'll just have to set off an avalanche on the Verte after the first fall of snow and go down on top of it on a surf board.'

'I've already told you that idea makes me wan't to puke!'

'I'm stumped ... I know, why don't you have a sex change, and do some big first-female ascent of a route you have already done as a man. That would create a big stir! You could call yourself Marinette. No other climber would have managed that one before you! And you should be able to corner the exclusive rights for ages.'

'Now you're taking the piss,' snarled Meriadoc.

'Right, go up the Italian side of the Matterhorn with a parapente and come down the North Face in a barrel.'

'I think that's already been done,' sighed Meriadoc. 'No . . . the public, the newspapermen, they need to be taken by surprise . . . to be really surprised! Get it?'

'That's it!' exclaimed Ethelbert suddenly. 'I've got the answer. The Tour du Mont Blanc!'

'What do you mean – Tour du Mont Blanc?' Meriadoc asked thoughtfully. 'Surely that isn't done any more? With all the impossible stunts people are racking their brains to invent, are there really any types left who want to just plod around Mont Blanc?'

'I believe so, I'm sure of it!' replied Ethelbert.

'But how should I do it? Backwards, or hopping on one foot?'

'No, quite the opposite. Make it absolutely simple. Take a week over it. Just the normal way. To prove that you're not only a demi-god, but also human like everyone else.'

'Perfect. Absolutely perfect! Great! It takes someone like you to dream up a ploy like that!'

The undertaking was a tremendous success. Accompanied by a few journalists, Meriadoc touched the heart of the crowds by the human side of his act. All the papers published the photo where, sitting by the edge of a path, his forehead bathed in sweat, he was dressing his blisters. It was the start of his real career.

THE LONDON DINNER

Strange as it may seem, its because the lightning had struck, high up on the North Face of the Aletschhorn, on 13 August of that year, that I found myself, on the first day of December, clad in a dinner jacket which didn't belong to me, driving by night across London through the late autumn fog.

The lightning had hit a party which, right from the start of the route, had been several rope-lengths ahead of us, having started from the Hollandia Hut whereas we had come from Konkordia. Nothing had forewarned us of the sudden arrival of the thunderstorm which, indeed, moved away again as fast as it had come. We got away, Jean-Claude and I, with a good shake up and a bad fright, but the other pair was closer to the ridge and was not so lucky. We climbed up to them in a fierce little hailstorm and found them in rather bad shape. One was British and the other German; both were suffering from slight burns. The German had lost his ice axe. The Brit had lost the use of one arm and had sprained an ankle: he had been hurled several metres down the slope and owed his life to the ice screw to which he had been belayed and which had held firm.

We were in a remote spot, and it would have taken too long to alert the mountain rescue. Besides, the two casualties wanted to carry on, and seemed just about fit enough to do so. We decided to rearrange the ropes: Jean Claude took the German under his wing, and I the Britisher. In this way we managed the rest of the face without too much trouble. Also the weather had turned fine again, and the whole situation appeared less dramatic than it had done earlier. We moved up the ridge together, but soon, as my rope was the slower of the two, I told the other pair to move on at their own pace and wait for us from time to time; it seemed pointless for them to stay always close to us.

Injured as he was, my partner climbed with plenty of spirit. He didn't even want to stop for any length of time, judging that his ankle would only become more painful as soon as it was no longer heated up by the exertions. I kept well above him so that I could check any slip, and thus had plenty of time to have a good look at him. He was a man in his forties, in whose lean face sparkled two large grey eyes. He wore the ragged clothes traditionally sported by the British: patched trousers, an ancient, faded sweater with frayed cuffs, a greenish cagoule, its rents and tears stuck together with crossed bits of sticking-plaster ... In the Metro you might have given him a small coin. But he spoke excellent French, and so I thought – I don't quite know why – that he must be an academic. It was just an idea that crossed my mind, but of course I had other things to do than ponder about his life history. The first priority was to reach a safe haven before nightfall.

It is 2500 metres down from the top of the Aletschhorn to Belalp, 2500 metres of ridges, snow slopes, glaciers, scree and mountain-paths at the end. It goes on forever ... Nevertheless, we were in time to catch the last cable-car, and there we found Jean-Claude's party waiting for us.

From here a complicated sequence of trains could have taken us to Grindelwald, but our British friend was generous enough to summon a taxi. He was feeling better and some movement had returned to his arm but, worn out by his big effort, he slept throughout the journey. We asked to be dropped off at Stechelberg where I had left my car, and there we took leave of our new friends. Poking about in a dusty pocket of his rucksack, my Briton extracted a wallet – a magnificent one, I can tell you – and pulled from it a visiting card which he gave me with his profuse thanks. I scribbled down for him my own address on the back of a hut receipt. And I wasn't half surprised when I took in, a bit later, both his name and his title: our ragamuffin was called Lord Whichunt.*

And that's why, having been invited by my new friend to the Annual Dinner of the Alpine Club, we were driving through London at the beginning of the following winter ...

I had arrived by air a few hours earlier, and had to leave again next day. It was a bit foggy but the weather was unseasonably mild, and we had the windows open. I had worked for two years in America and so my English was quite fluent, but I had never been to London. The city seemed enormous ... There were moments when I was startled by the left-hand driving but I was careful not to show it. I was also much entertained by the famous red two-storeyed buses, the large policemen with their extra tall helmets, the streets with their rows of dozens of identical houses, distinguished only by the colours of the front doors deep inside their pillared porticos. I was delighted to be there and to be about to take my place in the bosom of such an illustrious gathering: indeed I felt that I had entered the world of Phileas Fogg ...

* *Author's note:* This name is not a reference to Lord Hunt (of Everest reknown) but a family joke concerning a cousin of the author who is another Lord Hunt.

The dinner was held in a large building near the Thames, and we were directed to a hall on the ground floor where drinks were served. Here I had another surprise. I had been reflecting that I was about to join the most ancient of all alpine clubs, but it had not occurred to me that the people I would meet there would themselves be so ancient. By and by I was to discover the reasons for this. The cost of the dinner – or so I heard – was twenty-five pounds, and no doubt the younger members of the Club knew of better ways of spending such a sum. And then, it is in later years that one really likes to meet fellow-survivors of the passage of time.

At any rate, my host was – apart from myself – one of the youngest members present. He had warned me beforehand that he would not be able to be with me all the time, having duties to carry out in the Club, and I had assured him that I would have no problem in entertaining myself. And indeed, he was soon surrounded by people and carried off away from me, but I wasn't in the least bored. It was absorbing to study the crowd which thronged the room, mostly men in their dinner-jackets, more rarely ladies in long dresses. And this gathering was, dare we say it, of such a venerable age that it seemed hard to recognise the connection between so many worthy ancients and the rough reality of the sport of climbing. I just couldn't imagine that all these fragile patriarchs, squeezed into their gala outfits, could ever have been battling against the storm which lashed their anoraks, soaked in wet snow and stiff with ice... The only thing here that might conjure up the image of snow was the immaculate whiteness of the many heads of hair.

There was gin and sherry on offer. I took a gin-and-tonic and, glass in hand, steered through the crowd, trying to visualise the early life of the veterans I brushed past, seeking without success to put names to their faces. As time went on, I began to imagine that I could decipher various adventures written into those deep wrinkles and into the corner of a smile. I was particularly fascinated by a smallish greybeard who must have been close to a hundred years old. Firmly pressed against the serving table, talking to nobody, he concentrated on getting hold of the maximum number of sherries which he gulped down to the last drop and, as soon as he had put down one glass, he was already reaching for the next.

Having watched these goings-on for some time, I went to study the table-plan which was pinned up in a corner of the room. We were about a hundred and thirty diners: among them I recognised the Liechtenstein

Ambassador and various famous names in mountain history. One of these attracted my attention: that of James Eccles. In the second half of the nineteenth century there had been a well-known mountaineer of that name. Asking myself whether this could be one of his descendants, or whether it was a case of pure coincidence, I looked for Lord Whichunt to ask him about it, but he couldn't tell me. Doubtless this James Eccles must be some kind of great grandson or great-grand-nephew of the Victorian mountaineer for he was one of the Club's invited guests for the evening and was going to propose the last toast. But, apart from Colonel Edward Masonridge, who had been in contact with him but was unfortunately confined to bed this evening because of an attack of gout, nobody there knew anything about this James Eccles. Anyway, we would doubtless find out in the course of the last toast, and that would be enough to satisfy my curiosity.

Banging a little hammer to ensure silence, a master of ceremonies now informed us that dinner was served in a room on the third floor. At the same time he asked the young ones if they would be so kind as to leave the one and only lift for the use of the older guests. The young ones! It was, in truth, a weird doddering band which tackled the task of mounting the large stone staircase, doing their best to demonstrate by this heroic climb that some of their vital functions were not yet defunct. It was a moving sight, and I didn't dare think of the scene in the lift...

We looked for our places on the long tables, decorated with anemones, a group of waitresses, dressed in black with white aprons, watched our entrance with curiosity. The Reverend J.F.Tyndicott said Grace, after which we say down with a great shuffling of chairs. I was next to Lord Whichunt and, as soon as everyone had inspected the menu, I began to make contact with my other neighbours. One of them had been a member of Tilman's expedition to Everest, another had spent a whole summer working up at the Vallot Observatory without once coming down, a third seemed to have explored every single mountain on earth... The talk flowed easily, even if some hands cupped to ears were a reminder that hearing had not improved with the years... And I felt that I was myself a living part of a little piece of alpine history, when it was pointed out to me that yonder venerable diner, his shirt-front so stylishly adorned with little starched pleats was the last man to have seen Mallory and Irvine alive in 1924, or that this one, with a white beard reaching down to his bow-tie, had pioneered the first ascent of a route which, even today, was not often repeated.

From where I sat I could comfortably observe the small grizzled sherry-swigger. He had been amongst the last to slide into his seat on the top table, just as grace was being said, and since then he had not missed a single mouthful. Having guzzled with a healthy appetite the vol-au-vent which started the meal, he noticed that the lady next to him had not touched hers, and – having whispered a few words into her ear – he had, with a conjuror's skill, carried out a rapid switch of plates ... At the same time he was swigging the Chablis, beckoning to the waiter as soon as his glass was empty. Between courses he broke off pieces of bread, munching them with evident relish. I noticed that, on several occasions, his neighbours made efforts to engage him in conversation, but to no avail. The only response was a slight shake of the head which quickly discouraged all approaches. On the other hand, I was pleased to see him enjoying several helpings of his veal escalope with mixed vegetables. After the Chablis he took equal pleasure in the Château Camarsac which went with the main course, draining it to the last drop. For dessert he went straight to the apple-pie, dousing it with lashing of cream, and, when the liqueurs came round, he helped himself to a huge, brimful glass of Brandy. Here and there cigars began to appear in the dining room. Our friend pulled from his pocket a small pipe of distinctly antique design. The time for the after-dinner speeches had arrived.

The President dealt quickly with the first three toasts addressed respectively to Her Majesty the Queen, the members of the royal family and the Club's guests. This gave me a moment of intense inner-joy: contemplating the whole gathering as, upstanding, it declaimed with one voice 'The Queen', I pictured to myself the ribaldry and catcalls which would accompany a similar toast to the President of the Republic in any gathering of French mountaineers, be they ever so aged ...

The fourth toast, to the Principality of Liechtenstein, went on rather longer.

When it was on the point of finishing, my little elderly friend extinguished his pipe, leapt to his feet with vigour and, without a single note to assist his memory, started to propose the fifth toast, that of the Alpine Club.

The start was traditional: 'Your Excellency, my Lords, Ladies and Gentlemen ... '

And then, straightaway, he started to talk of mountains, real mountains, and – whether or not he was related to his illustrious namesake – it was obvious that he knew what he was talking about. The picture he drew for us of the early years of the Club was gripping, full of life. Never before had I understood so well the passion which had animated the first British alpinists.

The speaker recalled for us the long journey they had had to make, by boat, steam train and coach, to reach the Promised Land. He described in detail the primitive shelters that got established, one-by-one, around the fringes of the mountain ranges. He recounted the history of the fierce competition for the first ascents, and the battles amongst rival climbers for the services of the best Swiss or French mountain guides. He reminded us of the inadequacy of the early primitive equipment, the drawbacks of hobnailed boots, the fragility of long ice axes with wooden shafts, the permeability of hemp ropes which soaked up the water and then froze, going stiff as iron bars. He spoke of the trouble caused by that heavy white tent, which, on Whymper's advice, he had acquired for himself, only to find at the end of the day that it was more of a hindrance than a help.

I saw eyes opening wide in the audience. But stupefaction reached its height when James Eccles – for there could be no doubt about it, it was he himself, there amongst us in person – calmly undertook to tell us the tale of his first ascent of the Peuterey Ridge with the Payot brothers on 31 July 1877, giving us first of all some hitherto unpublished details about their two earlier attempts, and then reconstructing for us, with a superb flight of eloquence, the full story of this great climb, performed more than a century ago.

We felt we were on the climb ourselves ... We shivered with him in the icy cold of the bivouac ... We could see the blue splinters of ice, spraying out under the guide's ice-axe ... We balanced gingerly on the verglas that coated the rocks ... We suffered thirst because the water in the flask had run out ... And finally, we felt the deep emotion which came with the realisation that no further obstacles stood between us and victory ... Entranced, spellbound, we re-lived one of the great moments of alpine history.

James Eccles' eyes shone with pleasure as he described for us the relatively easy way through the big cornice which opened the way to Mont Blanc de Courmayeur ... And he finished his speech with an earnest appeal.

'And right on the summit of Mont Blanc,' he said, 'what do you think we found? The pure radiant whiteness of the peak? The unspoiled solitude of the mountains? The wild appeal of the heights? Not a bit of it! What awaited us on the top, which had been reached that day via the normal route by three big parties, complete with guides and porters, what we saw there was filthy snow, trampled all over by dozens upon dozens of boots, soiled with food scraps, refuse and bottles which nobody had taken the trouble to remove! And will you believe it that, in order to escape from that disgusting spectacle, we had to climb down again a bit on the Miage side, before we could enjoy our victory in a more welcoming spot. And that we said as a joke, but not without a touch of bitterness, that soon the Mont Blanc range would have to be submitted to inspections by the Health Department! And that was in 1877 ... So I now put the question to you – to you, the young. What have you really managed to do in the meantime to preserve the mountains in that pure, unspoiled state which is their essence? And what are you *now* going to do about it? Think about it. And whilst I am waiting I raise my glass to our dear old Club.'

'The Club,' repeated the audience, who had risen to their feet.

Silence fell, and James Eccles, his head raised a little, seemed still to be focusing his intense gaze on some snowy ridge or some corner of the sky. The assembly did not disturb his reverie, and we could all count the twelve strokes of midnight drifting in through the half open windows.

As soon as the last stroke had died away, James Eccles was no longer with us. He had suddenly dissolved, the way a light mist evaporates in the sun's rays.

And not one word could be heard as the guests, struck dumb to a man, slowly left the dining room.

On the staircase, Lord Whichunt was one of the first to regain his voice. He whispered in my ear: 'I do hope that you have enjoyed our old British customs.'

CARMENCITA

To the guides of Chamonix,
these imaginary guides.

The rain which had fallen the previous night had purified the atmosphere, as it were, and the fine weather seemed to be back for good. Flashing out from the lingering clouds, bright rays of sun spruced up the lawns and colourful flowerbeds, still spangled with little waterdrops. The air was full of the fragrance of warm, damp earth. Camille Portelaz, President of the Guides' Company, breathed it in deeply as he walked down the paved path which winds round the church, thinking, as he often did, that this was the prettiest part of the whole town. As he reached the old bell tower he looked up at the clock-face just as the midday Angelus was beginning to ring. Several idlers, standing around the wooden board erected for the display of the latest weather forecast, were consulting it. But on reaching the small square between the church and the former presbytery, Portelaz made for the latter, a large and handsome residence with an extensive roof of four slopes covered with green copper and thick walls pierced by narrow windows. It was now known as the Maison de la Montagne. He went in, walked down the stone corridor, and entered the Guides' Bureau.

'Hey, Camille,' said the chief guide, addressing him. 'There's a great fat letter come for you.'

Thus addressed, Portelaz held his hand out over the counter, and raised his eyebrows as he took the thick missive, covered with the multi-coloured stamps of a Latin American republic and sealed with five dabs of red wax on the back. The address ran:

Al Señor Presidente
del
'Chamonix Guides' Company'
y al legal oficial de la localidad
Monte Blanco Francia

The tall, black regular letters in which it was written had received an addition in blue ballpoint from an anonymous and intelligent post-office employee whose note suggested: 'Try 74400 Chamonix.'

'What does this *legal oficial* mean?' asked Camille.

'Maybe we ought to show it to the notary?' suggested the chief guide.

'Hold on!' said Achille Bletterans, who had witnessed the scene. 'The client I had yesterday was out there looking at the weather forecast a minute ago, and he's a lawyer. Why don't I ask him?'

Having inspected the envelope on all sides, Maître Ampon judged that it would indeed be better to open it in the presence of a sheriff's officer or a notary. An appointment was made to meet at the office of the latter personage that afternoon, before the men on duty changed shifts.

As a precaution, Camille Portelaz was accompanied by another guide, Étienne Vardesse, who could speak English pretty well, and his neighbour from the next chalet Manuel Rodriguez, a Spanish mason who knew not only his native language but enough French to provide a translation if necessary.

The notary broke the seals and opened the envelope, taking out a letter of fourteen sheets which, after a quick glance, he handed to Manuel Rodriguez.

That gentleman looked through them for the first time swiftly, frowning and moving his lips slightly as he read certain passages. His audience watched in attentive silence.

Then Manuel said, 'Madre de Dios!' and began reading the letter more closely. The summary he gave when he had finished struck everyone as important and peculiar enough for a Spanish teacher at the Jeanne d'Arc School to be asked to provide them with a complete and exact written translation. The notary put the document away in his safe for the night, and next morning the teacher started work on it, with the the aid of a clerk to help with legal terminology and a young trainee guide for questions of topography and mountaineering technique. Three days after the letter had arrived the translation was ready, and was handed over to Camille Portelaz.

We will not print the text of the missive, which had come to the Company from a distant village on the other side of the Atlantic and the other side of the Equator. To reproduce it in full, interesting as it might be to those curious about such matters, would demand too many typographical signs, and the details would strike some as a little tedious. But the essentials constituting the general gist of the document deserve analysis, for they summed up the entire earthly existence, the hopes, sacrifices and passions of Señora Carmen Montanchez Guadalquezar de Valmayor, recently deceased.

It had all begun long ago, when her father, the rich landowner Don Cristobal Montanchez del Santador Albariz Benaguacil, and her mother, Señora Trinidad Guadalquezar Navasces de Montanchez, had decided to celebrate the twentieth birthday of their beloved only daughter by taking the adolescent girl to the Old World on a long and magnificent tour. While the bustle of the great capitals of Europe and the luxury of their shops did not captivate the free daughter of the pampas, the visit to the Alps which was the culmination of the journey had left her with ineradicable memories. Carmen had done several climbs with Chamonix guides, and the revelation of the world of the high mountains had left its radiant stamp on her for ever. It had been hard to tear the girl away from her beloved peaks. She sobbed in the barouche taking the family to Geneva, and could calm down a little only by promising herself to come back some day.

But along came life with its inevitable succession of trials, burdens and duties. Carmen's parents, who were already elderly and fell ill soon after their return from Europe, wanted a protector for their beloved child and found one in the person of a worthy, rich and lonely widower, the nobleman Ignacio Valmayor de Tallarubias Zurramaga y Miravalles, who could guarantee his new wife all that could be wished for in the way of affection and security.

The following summer, therefore, saw not the return of the enthusiastic daughter of the Americas to the snow-covered peaks, but her wedding in the old baroque church of Tocatovilla. Her parents had acted wisely, for shortly afterwards they both died, without knowing the joys of dandling young heirs on their knees. And there never were any heirs. To their great grief, the couple remained childless, and devoted their time to the management of their vast estates. However, Carmen still dreamed of fulfilling her vow and making the long journey again. In her bedroom, below the ebony crucifix, the picture of the Madonna and the crystal stoup of holy water, she had placed an engraving bought in the year of that entrancing vacation, showing Mont Blanc and the entire range of the Aiguilles. This panorama sometimes distracted Señora Montanchez Guadalquezar de Valmayor during her devotions, but then again, it sometimes led her into happy meditations on the beauty of the Creator's works.

However, she had to care for the health of a dearly loved husband whose attacks of nephritis prevented him from undertaking long journeys. She had to help him administer the vast estates they jointly owned and an ever-growing fortune in securities. And one day she inevitably found herself alone, in long black widow's weeds, pursuing the task by herself.

Carmen's management, noted for its originality, was both so skilful and so charitable that her neighbours were soon taxing the saintly woman with Marxism, while the country's political agitators accused her of bourgeois imperialist paternalism. Taking no notice and going her own way, she remained active and alert, with an eye open for trouble, continuing her work along the same lines as before, expanding her business, gradually setting up the most meritorious of her farmers on their own account and ensuring that the rest received the training which would one day enable them to benefit fully by the same advantages. There could therefore be no question of going away for months on end to pursue an old dream in Europe. But an idea had taken root in her mind, and this idea comforted her and cheered her at difficult times.

She died peacefully and devoutly in her ninety-seventh year, and was greatly mourned. Her last will and testament made thousands of peons to whom she had left the land on which they had lived bless her name. And she had given her notary a long letter which he himself, as arranged, had addressed to the Chamonix Guides' Company.

To cut a long story short, Señora Carmen Montanchez Guadalquezar de Valmayor was leaving her entire fortune in securities to the Chamonix Guides' Company, on three conditions which she never for a moment thought might not be accepted with delight and gratitude.

The President of the Company called a meeting of the committee for next evening, also asking several patriarchs and sons or grandsons of former guides to attend. It was raining steadily, and everyone came, more particularly because it appeared that the reason for this speedily arranged meeting was something odd and important.

Camille Portelaz read out the translation of the letter in full, whereupon total silence fell, a silence broken only by old Alfred Coveray, who could not help exclaiming, 'Cor stone the crows!', a comment which faithfully enough summed up the general opinion.

The three conditions made by Señora Carmen Montanchez Guadalquezar de Valmayor were as follows:

1.   A room in current use, part of the Guides' Bureau was to accommodate the dead woman's favourite pieces of furniture, hangings, and various other decorative objects, along with her full-length portrait. All these items were already packed in large crates, and an aircraft

would be chartered to fly them in. A room measuring at least twenty square metres would be required.

2. The ashes of the noble donor would arrive in Europe on the same plane and would also be taken to Chamonix. A grand religious ceremony would be held in the church in memory of the dead woman; it was essential for all the guides to be present. The urn was to be carried by one of the men with whom she had once climbed, or failing that one of their descendants, who would also deliver the farewell speech.

3. Furthermore, a team of young guides would undertake to escort the dead woman up the fifty principal peaks of the massif by interesting routes. Thus she would fulfil in death the promise she had once made herself and could not keep while she was alive. The series of climbs was to end on Mont Blanc, where they were to dig down through the snow of the peak to the rock, and here, in a niche carved out of the rock and then sealed, the mortal remains of Carmen Montanchez Guadalquezar de Valmayor would lie awaiting the Day of Judgement and the Resurrection, protected from erosion and ice-falls, in the heart of the mountains she had known so little and loved so much.

'Better see what's in the jackpot first!' commented Félix à Montcoutant.

'Must be a tidy bit,' said Camille Portelaz. 'We want to think hard before saying no. The relief fund sometimes runs low. Remember Robert's widow Marie-Paule, left with her two kids? We could pay out sizeable grants for cases like hers ... and put some aside for pensions ... not to mention it's a dead person's wishes ...'

'Nobody's ever going to get Tibère Joucaz into a church. It's against his convictions!' whispered Paul Giuseppini to his neighbour, Alfred Coveray.

'If there's a pile of loot on offer, like they seem to be saying, you can bet your life I'll get him there, convictions or no convictions,' replied Coveray in the same tone. 'I'll kick him up the backside if I have to!'

'But carting that urn all round the place,' someone else objected. 'Thought about that, have you? I mean, who's going to take that job on and lose his season's earnings?'

'S'pose we should be thankful she got herself cremated!' sighed Jules Lafrasse. 'See yourselves carrying a coffin up and down the mountains?'

'How about a chopper?' someone suggested.

'No,' said Camille. 'The letter says clearly it has to be "interesting routes". She'd never have thought of going by chopper! Anyway, there weren't any helicopters in her day!'

They finally decided that if each guide, besides paying his dues to the Company, gave up a small percentage of his summer climbing fees, there would be enough to pay a team of two men, who could thus make fifty ascents without losing out on fair payment for their efforts.

'Doing the traverse of the Aiguilles in two days would make it eleven summits at a go!' remarked Étienne Vardesse.

'Depends if you count the Pointe Chevalier and the Pointe Lépiney among the "principal peaks of the range"!' observed Tibère Joucaz. 'If you don't it's only nine.'

'Still, that makes nine anyway!' replied Étienne. 'And another time you could do the Tour, the Purtscheller and the Javelle in a day, starting from the Albert Premier Hut; you could do the Forbes Ridge next day, the North Face of the Argentière the day after that, the Tour Noir the day after that, the North-East Face of the Courtes and the Ravanel/ Mummery the day after that ... then, starting from the Couvercle, it would take two days to climb the Ecclésiastiques, one day for the Verte, another day for the Droites, another for the Triolet and the Pointe Isabelle ... so in ten days you'd have climbed another seventeen ...'

'What a slog!' sighed Jacques à Montcoutant.

'But that'd still be half of 'em done!' said Étienne, amused by the game. 'We'd have to add the Dru, the Requin, the Aiguille de Roc, the Aiguille de la République, the Peigne, the Pélerins, the Deux Aigles, the Tacul and the Maudit, you could do those quick from the Aiguille du Midi, the Trident, the Capucin, the Tour Ronde, the Dent du Géant, the Aiguille de Rochefort, Mont Mallet, the Grandes Jorasses, the Petites Jorasses, the Dolent ... er ... the Aiguille de Talèfre ... the Aiguille de l'Éboulement ... let's see, the South Ridge of the Aiguille Noire. She wants an interesting route; well, I call that a bloody interesting route ... so that makes forty-seven ... And we could wind up with the Miages to Bionnassay to Mont Blanc traverse! It's in the bag!'

'In the urn, you mean!' Marcel Descharmoz corrected him, but the audience was too preoccupied to feel like laughing.

'Offering to do this round trip yourself, are you?' Camille asked Étienne Vardesse.

'Why not? Make a change from dragging halfwits around the Papillons! I'll go if Fanfan comes too!' he replied, turning to his cousin Florent Gaudenaz, known as Fanfan.

'Okay,' replied the latter. 'Consider it done!'

'How about Mont Blanc, though?' objected Paul Giuseppini. 'You're forgetting the Mont Blanc bit! Remember how thick the snow is before you get down to rock. Nobody knows just how thick! Thirty-five metres? Fifty metres? Who can say ... and with all those ecologists hot on our arses!'

This last was a weighty argument, and the company discussed it at length.

'If there's a sizeable party of us goes up one fine October day but we do it on the quiet, keep it to ourselves, there won't be any ecologists to notice us and wonder what we're doing!' said Alfred Coveray. 'The ones that come here in summer will be back home in town wasting paper and ink, you can bet, and nobody's going to tell them. But actually digging down through the snow, now that's a real problem, and a tricky one too!'

'How about a flame cutter? And a dynamo?' suggested Jules Lafrasse. 'We could put in a set of shafts, run casing so it wouldn't get stopped up again. We could use fixed ropes and jumars, work in relays, draining off the water ... Maybe we ought to ask the glaciologists for advice.'

'We don't want any strangers mixed up with this!' growled Achille. 'There's enough people know as it is, and the less it gets around now outside ourselves the better.'

There were murmurs of approval. In any case, this was only the beginning of July, and there was still plenty of time to solve the final problem. On the basis of a unanimous vote of all present bar one, the committee decided that it would quietly accept the offer made to it.

Camille Portelaz now set about searching the archives for the names of men who might have been guides to the noble señorita in her day. Unfortunately, they had all died, the last of them some time ago. But at least he found one of her former mule drivers. This was old Narcisse à la Floriaz, who had begun work with the mules when he was nearly fifteen, and had been with the Montanchez family during their visit. Narcisse à la Floriaz was now over ninety years of age, but in spite of his over-frequent recourse to the bottle he could still just about stand upright, and it was possible to envisage him carrying the urn. The drawback, however, was that he was rather gaga, and his alcoholic memory did not hold out much hope of a well-documented farewell speech.

'Remember when you were a lad with the mules?' he was asked.

'Don't I just, oh, don't I, though!' he replied in a somewhat tipsy voice, wiping away a tear.

'You went up the mountains with a foreign girl ...'

'Oh, sure, I remember that all right!' he exclaimed, suddenly waking up. 'She was a juicy little piece and no mistake ... a nice easy lay too! Blimey, don't I just remember! The fun and games we had, the two of us ... ooh, if I was to tell you the half of it ...'

The members of the committee who had come to sound him out preserved an embarrassed silence in the face of these unexpected revelations, which did not fit the idea they were beginning to form of the dead woman. Moreover, such remarks were a serious threat to the solemnity of the farewell speech.

'Gorblimey!' continued Narcisse, his eye lighting up, 'oh, gorblimey! Called me her little chickabiddy, she did. I'm telling you straight, she called me her little chickabiddy! She'd have got my soul damned, no error! What a cracker, oh wow, what a cracker! Gorgeous blonde, she was. From Sweden, I think ... no, I remember now, it was Finland. Cor, talk about hot stuff!'

A sigh of relief greeted the mention of the beautiful Finn.

'No, not that one!' they told old Narcisse. 'Kind of a Spaniard, she was. From South America. Most likely a brunette. She went climbing with guides.'

'Oh yes?' said Narcisse à la Floriaz vaguely, relapsing into tearful apathy. 'Yeah, could be I remember the one you mean ... 'Nother pretty girl ... dark, though, that's a fact. Dead keen on the mountains, she was ... not so much my type, see? But as for that other girl ... ah, what a little cracker!'

And they could get no more out of him.

The aircraft landed at Geneva a week after the committee had officially accepted, and the sealed crates containing the various items sent from distant America were taken to Chamonix by special van. They were opened in a hangar at the Pèlerins, in the presence of the delegation of eight guides assigned to the job. When everything was unpacked, those present exchanged startled glances. Before them lay hangings of red brocade enriched with heavy gilt fringes, tables in marquetry and niello work, chairs of exotic woods, dressers set with diamonds, caryatids holding up candelabras with turned sconces, chandeliers with glass drops, reliquaries of engraved crystal, alabaster and porphyry basins filled with precious stones, cameos, intaglios, pearls, opals, turquoises, moonstones, sapphires, emeralds, topazes and carbuncles, not to mention a baroque profusion of painted Virgins and chubby-cheeked cherubs blowing trumpets.

'We can't put this lot in the Bureau!' exclaimed Camille. 'I mean, what would we look like? It would send the clients running! They see us in a wild, virile, rugged setting ...'

'The common room?' suggested Jacques à Montcoutant.

A great sigh of approval greeted this ingenious idea, for the common room was certainly part of the Bureau, as stipulated, but it was strictly private. It is in this room that the guides decide what climbs they will do next day, on the basis of the clients' requirements but out of their sight.

Almost unknown to all, the common room thus became the most extraordinarily luxurious place in the whole valley. A kind of lock area with three metal-clad doors, which themselves were separated by thick draperies of local loden cloth, masked the Gothic arch of the old doorway so that no profane eye should light upon the mysteries of this new Holy of Holies. Later on, the members of the Company annually knew moments of delirious pleasure when they saw the expressions on the faces of the newly promoted trainee Chamonix guides as they entered the place for the first time. The name 'common room', moreover, soon went out of general use, and was replaced by the more evocative title of Scheherazade's Chamber, entirely incomprehensible to the uninitiated. A number of clients were surprised to hear their guides, meeting on a moraine, exchange such remarks as 'See you in Scheherazade's Chamber this evening?', and credited them with an exciting night life which took them into secret dens of vice.

The truth was very different, for in the middle of the main wall of the Chamber hung the portrait of Carmen Montanchez Guadalquezar de Valmayor, painted when she was a handsome woman of around fifty, in all the brilliance and vigour of her maturity. Forceful, majestic, in her prime, the beautiful South American dominated her setting. A simple brown dress with a contrasting collar of Venetian lace clung to her rounded figure, which was firm and still pleasing to the eye, but it was chiefly her face which caught your attention, for the painter had given her that look which seems to follow you round the room wherever you may be, and the ironic and affectionate way in which Carmen looked down at her friends the guides swiftly made anyone with some peccadillo on his conscience feel uneasy. One man might take to paying his dues more regularly, another returned a piece of land which had been dividing his family for decades to a collateral branch, a third discovered the advantages of conjugal fidelity, and a great many gave up the deplorable practice of making clients miss out the summit at the end of the route: all this rather than feel awkward about facing their benefactress's penetrating eye. In fact the moral standards of the Company rapidly reached heights never before equalled.

The furnishing of the common room, however, fulfilled only the first of the three clauses. The religious ceremony prescribed in the second had been arranged for the afternoon of August 14th, to precede the solemnities at the Argentière cemetery and the big ball that evening. It was the best date to get all the guides assembled without overloading their traditional day of festivities on August 15th. The absolute necessity of everyone's attendance had been emphasized. A number of old gentlemen, almost contemporaries of Narcisse à la Floriaz, were pleased to be summoned so urgently to the gathering, and took their old mothball-scented uniforms out of the wardrobe with emotion. However, the lips of Tibère Joucaz had curled in a mocking smile at the repeated issuing of the summons. No doubt about it, he was planning to be ill and thereby display his anti-clerical convictions. But Alfred Coveray, as he had promised, took the matter in hand and invited the rebel to supper on the evening of the 13th, with a view, he said, to showing him his father's old guide's notebook, which Tibère had long wanted to see.

'You'll have a little drink?' he immediately suggested.

'Just a small one!' said Tibère. 'There'll be more than enough of that tomorrow ... and I'm supposed to be welcoming the nobs the day after.'

'My wife made this specially for us!' begged Alfred, who had indeed helped her to concoct a strange cocktail in which vodka vied with gin and whisky with champagne. 'Look, there's mint leaves in it, and I topped it up with a drop of orange juice ... all vegetarian, when you come to think of it. That'll slip down like mother's milk, that will, and won't do you much more harm.'

It has to be admitted that the concoction was excellent, and after several glasses Tibère Joucaz sat down at the Coverays' table in a very good mood, ready to do justice to a carefully prepared meal washed down successively by bottles of Sauternes, Corton Charlemagne, Pommard and Château Grillet. He proved himself a brilliant conversationalist, told tales of his youth, his early memories of the mountains, and even, by the time dessert was reached, some of his amorous exploits. It was after midnight when they left the table and Alfred suggested trying an old plum liqueur given him by his uncle the home distiller, which he brought out only on very rare occasions. Although more prudent in his own libations, the master of the house ended up rather too full of *joie de vivre*, and at two in the morning Madame Coveray, who had been told to keep a weather eye open, had to use all the eloquence at her command to prevent the two men from going to take a nocturnal dip in the icy springs of the Arveyron. They consoled themselves by singing the *Marseillaise* with much feeling, and swore eternal friendship, in honour of which they uncorked a bottle of champagne. After that Madame Coveray succeeded in laying them out side by side on the divan, where they fell into a deep sleep. Then, faithfully obeying instructions, she woke her husband about noon, left a pot of black coffee beside him, and went to Tibère Joucaz's home to fetch his official guide's uniform. When the time came, they had a certain amount of difficulty in getting its owner up on his feet and into it. Alfred, who was beginning to feel better, grimly prepared for the final trial, determined to boot his colleague into the procession if necessary, as he had promised, to make sure that no one could claim the will was null and void. But Tibère, no doubt still extremely drunk, put up no resistance.

'Where you taking me all rigged out like thish?' he inquired.

'To the ceremony for Señora Montanchez!' announced Alfred fiercely. 'And by God, you're going!'

'You bet I am!' agreed Tibère, apparently much moved by this notion. 'If there'sh one thing in life I regret it'sh never knowing Carmen. Good ol' Carmen! I'd do anything for her, I'm telling you shtraight!'

He subsequently amazed all his neighbours by the composure of his attitude, and spent the greater part of the funeral mass on his knees.

Finally, they awaited Narcisse à la Floriaz's farewell oration, which had been carefully written for him in advance and handed over amidst attempts to make him understand the importance of his mission.

'Your Reverence, your honour the Mayor, friends!' he began reading with concentration. 'I remember as if it were yesterday the intrepid daughter of the pampas, who so loved the mountains, and whom I had the honour of escorting when she set off to climb our Chamonix peaks . . .'

His scornfully dismissive look passed unnoticed by the spectators, and he continued conscientiously reading his text to the final peroration: 'Carmen! You have returned to our mountains. I always hoped you would. Welcome among us!'

He then slipped the piece of paper into his jacket pocket, and tried to take advantage of the fact that everyone was listening to do equal honour to the memory of his beautiful Finn.

'I could tell you about another nice little piece, though, couldn't I just!' he offered, but he was swiftly interrupted by Camille Portelaz, who was standing beside him.

The ceremony thus passed off very well in every way, validly fulfilling the second condition.

By now the urn had climbed forty-two peaks in the massif, taking routes which were often exceptionally interesting. It had chalked up seventeen north faces, abseiled a hundred and twenty-one times, bivouacked five times, and even made four first ascents, acquitting itself so well that the Diamond Chough award, bestowed by the Guides' Company on their best clients, was made next day to Señora Montanchez Guadalquezar de Valmayor, posthumously, of course. Yet again, all this had not been done without difficulty. Carmen's ashes were contained in a decorative urn made of an alloy of silver and copper, handsomely engraved in the rococo style, but weighing a good six kilos. It was protected from possible bumps by a polystyrene cover, the whole thing taking up a relatively large volume of space for the planned climbs. Étienne Vardesse and Florent Gaudenaz found it posing problems as soon as they prepared their equipment for the traverse of the Chamonix Aiguilles, the first route on the itinerary.

'Look here, old girl, you're bloody well going in!' cursed Fanfan, trying to fit the urn into his purple rucksack, the very latest model. 'As if you hadn't made enough fuss and bother for us already, and now you won't cooperate! Christ! Would you believe it? And I've nothing bigger to take her in.'

After several useless efforts, he had to resign himself to going up to the attic for a huge grey canvas expanding sack which had belonged to his grandfather.

'Really trendy you look!' remarked Étienne wittily.

'We have to take turns carrying her, don't forget!' snapped his cousin. 'The old cow! How come I ever got mixed up in this?'

'Get a move on, Fanfan!' grunted his friend. 'We accepted, and now we have to get on with the job. Let me tell you, this is no fun for me either.'

If the atmosphere had been unenthusiastic when they set off, it was extremely glum at their first bivouac on the Col du Fou. The temperature was icy, and when packing his new sack Florent Gaudenaz had forgotten to put the billies in. After a long day's climb they had no way of heating soup or even making a little tea, or of cooking the noodles supposed to be on the menu. They could only munch bread and bacon and suck snow, with the camping stove they could not use mocking them where it stood on a nearby ledge. The two men tried in vain to find a substitute for the billycan, but it was hopeless. Nothing would do.

'I'm cold! I'm hungry!' grumbled Étienne.

'There *is* a solution,' suggested Florent. 'We take the old lady out, put her in a plastic bag, all neat and tidy, so as not to lose a speck of her, and then we use the urn to make soup.'

'You're crazy!' protested Étienne.

'I'm not, I'm just practical. After all, it's the only container we have. We can scrub it out once we get down and put her back inside, plus a little bit of welding.'

'Nothing doing!' said Étienne emphatically.

'Well then, stop complaining! The old girl's really got my back up. Or down, rather; I reckon this bloody sack's given me curvature of the spine. Got my back up? I'm fed to the teeth! I've had her up to here! I can't stand those whims and fancies old folk take into their heads. I'm not climbing like this tomorrow. Tell you what, I'll just chuck her down, and that'll be it! Where is she? Where is she, then? Let me chuck her down!'

'You watch your step, Fanfan! I'm warning you. You chuck her down and I'll chuck you down after her.'

The night passed in an atmosphere of deep mutual antipathy. But next day's sunlight cheered the two men's spirits, and when they stopped at the Rognon des Nantillons, having come back down the Grépon after completing the entire traverse, a certain euphoria took hold of them.

'Nine!' said Fanfan jubilantly. 'Nine peaks! I hope you're satisfied, Spanish lady!'

And thus, as climb followed climb, a growing familiarity arose between the noble benefactress and her guides. From describing her as 'the old girl' they soon passed, with a certain degree of inaccuracy, to calling her 'the Spanish lady'. They soon decided it would be more polite to call her Señora Carmen, went on to Carmen, and ended up with the more intimate and affectionate diminutive Carmencita.

'Here, give me Carmencita today!' one of them would say in the morning. 'I don't like to be without her. I need to feel her close.'

'Well, Carmencita, enjoy that, did you?' the other would enquire in the evening. 'Pretty good north face, that one! I believe this is only the third time a woman ever climbed it!'

With fine weather on their side, Étienne and Florent had made the ascent of forty-two peaks of the Mont Blanc range in little more than a month. Among them, most notably, were the ascent of the Grandes Jorasses by the Croz Spur, the Cornuau/Davaille on the Droites, the American Direct on the West Face of the Dru, the North Face of the Blanche de Peuterey, and a great many others as well. But they did not stop at that. They had surreptitiously taken their client over the Swiss frontier, so that she could also climb Monte Rosa, the Lyskamm by the Neruda route, the Italian ridge on the Matterhorn, the Jungfrau, the North Face of the Mönch, and the Mittellegi Ridge of the Eiger. Furthermore, in France they had opened four modern rock routes christened respectively, with more or less relevance – The Aztec Pyramid, The Treasure of the Incas, Olé-olé, and of course Carmencita.[1] They felt quite sad as they saw the day which would separate them from their lady friend approach, although not all their adventures had been without danger, for the mountains are dangerous places. Carmen had fallen twice, and the second time almost ended her posthumous existence not at the top of Mont Blanc but at the bottom of a crevasse on the Frêney Glacier. Never mind, she had been retrieved, and on 14 August there she was, safe and sound, if one may put it that way.

In the days following the Guides' Festival she completed the ascent of several peaks and various routes still missing from her list: the Frendo Spur, the Gervasutti Pillar, the North Face of the Dolent, the North Face of the Triolet, the West Face of the Petites Jorasses, the East Face of the Capucin, the South-East Ridge of Mont Maudit, and the traverse of the Aiguilles du Diable. For good measure, Étienne Vardesse and Florent Gaudenaz took her for a climb in Oisans and Bernina and initiated her into a Tyrolean traverse in Les Périades, and after that they left her to rest until the end of September.

The final phase of the operation was carried out on a suitable day after Jules Lafrasse had managed to find documentation on the drilling of the permafrost for oil in Siberia. According to him, if you hired a helicopter and took up a powerful generating set, a steam nozzle and a special drill, you could soon get through the thickness of the ice and as much rock as necessary below it. They all contributed towards the

[1] My thanks to Michel Piola for naming a new route on the Aiguille du Peigne Carmencita, after this story.

expenses of the enterprise, making an unsuccessful attempt to use French equipment, but after long proceedings and the filling in of multiple forms, it turned out that the rules were too complex to allow such a thing. Luckily Italy was not far off, and thanks to the flexibility of the official systems (or the elasticity of the red tape) on that side of the Alps they managed to hire the necessary equipment and a helicopter to transport it on a certain weekend in early October. All the men of the Company were anxious to be there to say their last farewells to Carmencita, and although there were some problems with the drilling it was successful in the end. Once in place, the drill swiftly made its way through the ice and cut a roomy cavity in the rock. Carmen was let down into this on the end of a nylon rope before the opening was sealed with a little concrete, which had to be mixed with boiling water because of the bitter cold. Then Camille Portelaz delivered the final speech in the name of all of them, in a few words of moving simplicity.

'Take care, Carmencita!' he said. 'See you!'

And more than one mountaineer furtively wiped away a tear, while Étienne Vardesse and Fanfan Gaudenaz did not even try to hold back their sobs.

Then they went back down to drink to the posthumous health of their benefactress, and the success with which her last wishes had been carried out.

Since that day, there have been rumours of mysterious incidents on Mont Blanc. People are surprised to find that the storm seems to restrain its fury when the Chamonix guides are in the area, and it is even said that unexpected rays of sunlight pierce the clouds to light them on their way. People are beginning to say, in low whispers, that Carmencita was a saint, citing, among a great many other signs and some miraculous cures on the Aiguille du Goûter, the surprising conversion of Tibère Joucaz, struck by the Faith during the funeral mass to which he had gone in a state one would have thought unlikely to attract celestial goodwill. It is whispered that a case may be presented in Rome for the beatification of one who might eventually become St Carmen of Chamonix, whereupon Mont Blanc would become the most elevated place of pilgrimage in Europe, ensuring the guides of a generous clientèle for ever. And surely Carmencita would not cease to dispense an abundance of grace and favour on the massif itself and the surrounding valleys.